Forgotten Work

ALSO BY JASON GURIEL

Technicolored

Pure Product

The Pigheaded Soul:
Essays on Poetry and Culture

Satisfying Clicking Sound

Forgotten Work

A Novel

Jason Guriel

BIBLIOASIS
Windsor, Ontario

FIRST EDITION

Library and Archives Canada Cataloguing in Publication

Title: Forgotten work / Jason Guriel.
Names: Guriel, Jason, 1978– author.
Identifiers: Canadiana (print) 20200230441 | Canadiana (ebook) 2020023045X
    ISBN 9781771963824 (softcover) | ISBN 9781771963831 (ebook)
Subjects: LCGFT: Novels in verse.
Classification: LCC PS861.U74 F67 2020 | DDC C813/.6—dc23

Simultaneously published in a hardcover limited edition of 300 copies, signed and numbered by the author.

Edited by Amanda Jernigan
Copy-edited by Emily Donaldson
Text and cover designed by Ingrid Paulson

Excerpts from *Forgotten Work* have appeared in *The Walrus*, *The Hopkins Review*, *The Dark Horse*, and *The Manchester Review*.

This is a work of fiction. Names, incidents, and characters are either the products of the author's imagination or, where real-life figures, products, or publications appear, used in a fictitious manner. Any resemblance to actual persons, living or dead, or actual events is purely coincidental.

Published with the generous assistance of the Canada Council for the Arts, which last year invested $153 million to bring the arts to Canadians throughout the country, and the financial support of the Government of Canada. Biblioasis also acknowledges the support of the Ontario Arts Council (OAC), an agency of the Government of Ontario, which last year funded 1,709 individual artists and 1,078 organizations in 204 communities across Ontario, for a total of $52.1 million, and the contribution of the Government of Ontario through the Ontario Book Publishing Tax Credit and Ontario Creates.

PRINTED AND BOUND IN CANADA

For

Henry, whose naps produced this book

and

Christie, the other half of the couplet

"I had no idea that anyone today still knew my *Wanderings*." The old gentleman stared into space—"Even I haven't thought of them, it's been so long since I thought of them. For years, I've been so far from any of these things, so far."

Herr Wolfgang Meier smiled delicately. "It hasn't escaped my, or, I should say, *our*, attention, dear sir, that you haven't committed anything to print for a long time, something that surprised and saddened us. And it was, after all, just chance that led us—though here I can probably say *me*—to discover your exquisite book, so to speak, anew."

Saxberger found the words he heard singularly moving. Was this young man really speaking about him? Was it truly possible that this young man, a complete stranger, knew about him and his forgotten work?

—*Late Fame*, Arthur Schnitzler

Prologue.

Like all young bands, they bandied names about
All evening. Lou, the lead guitar, liked "Lout,"
A word that clubbed you like a cord of wood.
It's dumb, said Lou, but arty dumb, like blood-
Smeared dolls deployed as drumsticks—Henry Rollins
Does Dada. Jim, on keys, preferred "The Dolphins,"
After the folk-rock ballad by Fred Neil.
Neil's was the sort of myth that would appeal
To men like Jim. His lungs were honeycomb,
His low voice, ladled out. A man must roam
Was Neil's recurring theme. He wrote a few
Great songs, swore off recording, then withdrew
To Xanadu (read: Florida). In exile
For several decades, Neil would not defile
His myth by adding even one more note
Of music to his oeuvre. Like a boat
That's washed its hands of waves but wants to keep
A churning world in view, he chose to sleep
Near water. Sometimes Neil would walk along
The shoreline. Sometimes he would aim a song
At dolphins. Basically, he beached himself,
His rumoured last recordings on a shelf
And out of earshot. But his profile, prow-

Like, always faced the sea.
                              "I think that's how
Great artists—or great bands—should be," said Jim,
As if inside an auditorium
And not his unnamed band's rehearsal space.
"They should be hermits, right? They should efface
Themselves." Because he led the group—composed
Its songs—Jim sometimes went full lecture mode.

"Like take The La's, who put out very little
Product," said Jim. The La's had dared to whittle
At one album for two years, the main
Songwriter, Mavers, plagued by sounds his brain
Contained. He tried and tried, but couldn't seem
To get on tape the contents of the dream.
The dreamer ran through personnel, requested
Miracles: a "'6os mixing desk."
One *was* supplied, but Mavers wanted pixies;
The mixing desk, he said, was missing '6os
Dust.
         The record company relieved
The La's—connoisseurs of dust, aggrieved
Auteurs—of all the tape amassed to date.
(The takes the band had cut were clearly great
Enough.) A twelve-track album saw release.
It was acclaimed. It was a masterpiece.

But Mavers, thwarted father, disavowed
His child. Much like Neil, he somehow wowed
The world against his will, then stopped recording.
Much like Neil's, his genius was for hoarding.

Both lives proved a lesson: less is more
Than what most artists try to bargain for.

"'And I am made more beautiful by losses',"
Added Jim. He sighed. "That's Howard Moss's
'Pruned Tree'." (Jim liked quoting poetry.)
An editor, Moss knew that shears can free
A shape from shaggy chaos; that life requires
Edits; that first drafts should be filed in pyres;
That most of what we make—not just the rough
Work—should be aired in public, puff by puff,
By way of chimney. Artists need more patience.
They flood the market, drown their reputations.

"Of course," said Jim, "we need a hit before
We vanish and become the stuff of lore."
Silence. And then: "I'm just not sure," said Lou,
"That I'm a dolphin." Everyone laughed—Jim, too.

Jim's space, a cramped garage they'd come to hate,
Was like a coop designed to incubate
An attitude: you have to learn to thrive
In limits. Jim had even had to hive
Off half the space; a wall of boxes, stacked
Like Marshall amps, deterred (by literal fact
Of matter) arms inclined to windmill widely.
It boxed the singer in; he couldn't idly
Wander off and roam the room the way
A star, unmoored from mic stand, starts to stray
From band, or buoys himself upon the surf
Of upturned palms, or strolls the stadium turf

To single out and touch a lone fan's hand
As frond-like arms brush by. Jim hadn't planned
To pen his band like veal, of course; his boxes
Had no other home. But paradoxes
Made him think. He liked the thought that jail
Produced a form of freedom; that a wail
Within a cell, hemmed in by razor wire,
Could be song.
                              Nabokov's book *Pale Fire*
Was his favourite art. If you behead
"This centaur-work" ("half poem, half prose," as said
By Mary McCarthy), leaving for the vultures
The torso (prose), what's left is Western culture's
Sharpest verse, by one John Shade. It dared
To rhyme and scheme. (Most poets now are scared
To seem traditional or scan as staid.)
The author, though, was fake. Behind "John Shade,"
Nabokov lurked like Oz. His book required
He fabricate a poet the world admired,
Which meant Nabokov had to ghostwrite first-
Rate verse.
                          He proved great art can be coerced.
To write about a brilliant poet, Nabokov
Had to be one. What a feat: to knock off,
'Cause your novel needs it, verse to order.
It's almost like a painter needs a border,
A poet needs a beat. It's almost like
The most confining place to place a mic
Is where a restless man, weighed down with wings
To stretch, should force himself to stand and sing.
Perhaps his cramped garage-cell might inspire,
Thought Jim. And then: "How 'bout the name 'Pale Fire'?"

The band had yet to settle on a sound,
Never mind a name. Their common ground
Was comically vast in terms of time and styles.
They could agree on Mozart, Dylan, Miles,
And Beatles, not to mention bass harmonica
Solos (see *Pet Sounds*); '60s electronica
(The talk of vintage robots: blips and bloops);
On talking blues and Talking Heads; on loops
Of samples softwared flush together; human
Minds together in one room, their acumen
Their only software as they improvise
On standards. (That's how jazzmen ionize:
They play and get a charge off one another.)

Stevens, poet, said that death's the mother
Of beauty. Jim's band thought obscurity
The thing. (A true fan proved his purity
By prizing the obscure, which signified
Authentic art.) Thus minor men who died
Before their time lived on inside the minds
Inside Jim's band. They loved James Booker, blind
In one eye, black, and gay—a man, the kids
Might say, positioned point-like on a grid
Where four identities had intersected.
One took spot-lit centre stage: neglected
Artist. Booker's hands, the way they fell
Upon piano keys, suggested Hell
Had sold him genius for a soul-shaped jewel
And lit a fire underneath his stool.
New Orleans-born, he played so fast and loud
He blurred into the sort of cartoon cloud

That's armed with surplus arms. He was a star
In Europe; stateside, in a bleak ER,
He died awaiting care for renal failure.

The French, of course, thought Welles was cinema's saviour.
But in the States, his voice supplied an earth-
Sized robot's gravity. To know your worth
And yet to be condemned to cartoon voice
Work—or, in Booker's case, your Sophie's choice
Of cloistered club to fade away in—is
An awful fate. "Do not be branded whiz
Kid or a wunderkind" would be one lesson.
Having peaked at metrical expression
In his youth, and stranded on Parnassus,
Daryl Hine could only watch as asses
Like Allen Ginsberg stormed the world below,
While Hine, basecamped with gods, acquired snow.

Another lesson: ending on a high,
Well-loved, is no way for a man to die.
Welles knew this. "How they'll love me when I'm dead,"
The washed-up wunderkind is said to've said.

* * *

Rehearsal talk would often turn to Blake,
Which meant, in Music Nerd, the late Nick Drake,
Who cut his starkest songs without his label
Knowing. He was a figure out of fable;
Drake, it's said, appeared one afternoon
And left the master tape for his *Pink Moon*—
A master's final record—with reception,
Then vanished. One part truth and one deception:

Drake, in fact, decided he would linger
For some tea. But yes, the flighty singer
Left a tape, a work of art entrusted
To the front-desk girl—an act encrusted
With import. Interpretation. Maybe
Drake, a desperate parent, left his baby
Orphaned with this girl so as to sever
Man from music. Maybe art is never
Finished—just abandoned to the gallery.

"That Wilde?" asked Lou.

                Jim shook his head. "No, Valéry."

Birth was brief; *Pink Moon* was cut in two
Nights with a single engineer in lieu
Of well-stocked studio. Perhaps a star
Shone overhead.

           "That album has guitar,
His voice, that's it," Lou marvelled.

                    "And," said Jim,
"Piano. Just a bit."

              The music, hymn-
Like, found few pews. In fact, it was dismissed.
"It could be that Nick Drake does not exist
At all," wrote one reviewer (*Melody Maker*).
Drake's voice—like sound that's taken shape, like vapour—
Bloomed, then frayed, and fractalled into air.
He was, his critics felt, just barely there.
Sometimes a man can seem less whole, less definite,
Than he is. The moon, when full, looks desolate,
More hole than hunk of rock, as if punched clean
Into the heavens.

Amitriptyline—
The drug that Drake was given for depression—
Stopped his mouth; it was his last expression,
In 1974. In time, of course,
A cult cohered, his name invoked with force
By men like Lou and Jim for whom "Nick Drake"
Had come to mean a more "authentic ache."

* * *

"Snobby bandmates wanted," Jim's ad sneered,
Its bottom scissored into fringe: a beard
Which each of them had plucked Jim's landline from.
(He wanted peers with teeth; the ad was chum.)

"Well, maybe we should call ourselves 'Pale Snob',"
Said Hal, half-crouched and futzing with a knob;
He treated his guitar amp with the care
A burglar, stethoscoped, will bring to bear
On tricky combination locks. He played
The bass and really didn't like to wade
Into debates. As one half of the rhythm
Section, he felt he shouldn't widen schisms
By wedging in yet more opinion. (Bedrock—
Unless, of course, the five-piece is in deadlock
And must break a tie—is what the guy
Who mans the bass should be.) He was a shy
And monk-like source of learning—erudition—
On the session man. The lost musician.

In general, Hal loved the so-called "genius
Of the system." Ford, say. Hawks. His thesis
Was about directors who'd resigned

Themselves to making pictures while confined
In studios. These scrappy hacks had voices.
Since their editors made garish choices,
Frugal men like Ford and Hawks were sly
And filmed no more than needed. This is why
A Ford, deciding that he'd got the shot,
Would cup the lens—"That's enough"—and blot
The world with one engorged Godzilla hand.
Such eclipses mean no more was planned
And what you see is all I ever meant
To say. The studio, stymied, couldn't dissent.
(It's not like extra footage or a different
Ending existed.)
                        Thus Ford left his imprint.
Westerns came to be confessionals
In which true craftsmen, gruff professionals
For hire, disclosed the contents of their heart
By proxy. Similarly, pop songs, art
By other means, demanded artistry.
Those beehived girl-group singers—"he kissed me"
Would be their major theme—were media
Through which producers channelled arias
For teens. In certain moods, Hal liked to state
That union men, like gold, were worth their weight
In scale. That image, from a poem he'd found
Online, summed up his thoughts: a holy sound,
An angel's, *can* have impure origins.
Collection plates must coexist with hymns.

Side note: those quotes that grip "authentic ache"
Were shapes Hal's fingers often liked to make
When Lou or Jim got going on the "real"

Thing or the way some artists make you feel
As if they're "pure," not "packaged." (See Nick Drake.)

* * *

"That wasn't bad," said Jim. "But one more take."
They'd been rehearsing Kurt Cobain's "About
A Girl," when Lou, inspired, brought up "Lout."

Dennis said, "Let's go again." He'd drawn
His mic cord from the freehand tangle on
The floor. Hal's fingers found their finger rests.
Lou toed an FX pedal as one tests
Cold surf.
            Dennis, who provided vocals,
Felt that music should sound wet and woeful.
Sometimes he recorded in the rain-
Coat of an ex: an item from the reign
Of Thatcher. Snares, he felt, should go off like
Old rifles. It should sound as if the mic
Has been positioned in a cavernous room
Inside an empty warehouse stocked with gloom,
The distant walls repeating each report
The drummer makes. The bass should be distorted,
Hi-hat hissing like a gas line leaking.
The singing should be half-hysterical speaking,
A croon to which a pair of trodes is clipped.
(Think Ian Curtis. David Byrne.) Equipped
With dour streak, he was a connoisseur
Of makeup, Converse, Morrissey, The Cure.

* * *

(And still inside its box, the band's unseen
Fifth member was a well-loved drum machine,
Which Jim had outbid others for online
And which, for now, would do to keep the time.)

* * *

Jim also loved *Pale Fire* because, in part,
It was about a man perfecting art.
(Fictional artists come to represent
The artists that we aren't.) Some will invent—
Perhaps because they can't achieve perfection—
Perfect works to house in works of fiction.
Take the critic Lester Bangs, who made
A bio for a minor band that played
A dirty, harp-hoarse strain of rock (garage).
The bio, masterful, was pure mirage;
Although the band, Count Five, had had the one
Hit song in this, the one real world, Bangs spun
A spurious account: a counter-canon
Recorded in a world that didn't happen,
But a world that Bangs willed into being
Very nearly real.
                        It can be freeing
To imagine (mind a studio space)
Bizarro art. In Coetzee's book *Disgrace*,
An English prof, disgraced protagonist,
Dreams up an opera. He's a fabulist,
Who knows his bogus piece is not to be

Performed. And yet he spurns reality,
Composes parts for banjo. Singing dog.
(Dreaming's better; making art's a slog.)

Fiction's greatest bard, from Jim's perspective,
Was the woman in *The Savage Detectives*,
Just out in English. Lost, with one piece to
Her name, she somehow draws a cult: a few
Men prize a copy of the small, obscure
Lit mag in which the poet (far too pure
To author more than one work) once appeared.
The men set out to find her. So revered
Is she it doesn't matter that the piece
She "wrote"—a group of lines that start to crease
And EKG into a choppy wave—
Is wordless; no, their zeal for her is grave
And boundless. (Had her poem *had* some words
Their fandom might've waned.)

                                                    Perhaps two thirds
Of all art ever made is hanging on
The drywall inside dreamscapes, or is drawn
In chalk upon the caves made when we close
Our eyes, or holds its breath like embryos
In deep freeze. Restless, Jim would often think
About unrealized work: the phantom ink
In which unwritten poetry is written.
Take Peter Van Toorn. This poet had a vision,
Wrote his one book, *Mountain Tea*, and never
Wrote another. More Van Toorn, however,
Could be dreamed.

                                        Jim also loved to think
About the band his band was on the brink

Of being. As a Frankenstein will suture
Fragments—that's how Jim conceived the future,
Piecing together life from other lives.
His band would have its hits. Its trophy wives.
Its text-poor, obfuscating liner notes.
Its self-indulgent soloing that bloats
The way a boa will and starts to swallow
Songs. Its dawning sense that fame is hollow.
Its getting back to basics—voice and bass,
Guitar and drums, fleshed out by silent space
Like stark displays of bones in galleries.
Its petty fighting over salaries.
Its wasted drummer, drifting off to drown
In puke. Its trying to update its sound,
Then swearing off the Pro Tools and embracing
Tape. Its starting over and erasing
False starts—

1.

Hubert's favourite work was *Mountain Tea*.
It's why he'd gotten into poetry.
He loved a stylish sentence. Strong vibratos.
He loved that Amis book about castratos,
The one that has a character called "Hubert."
He loved to say he loved the works of Schubert.
Most of all, he loved to love great books.

His earnest views, though, often earned him looks
Of pity. Books are "texts," and love? All wrong.
The point of reading (someone paused, mid-bong,
To tell him) isn't pleasure or escapism;
The point is pointing out the hidden racism,
Sexism, and/or classism of the text—
Which left the English major feeling vexed.
He'd found himself inside the sort of dorm
Where young men, parroting their profs, perform
The part of well-read mind and talk 'til dawn
Of Butler, Derrida, Foucault, Lacan,
And other luminaries of the Left.
But Hubert, waving off the bong, soon left.
A life-sized holo Scarface followed him,

Machine gun swivelling.

                    At home, his dim

Room, sensing movement, raised the lights a notch.

To raise his spirits, Hubert liked to watch

The sort of film his classmates liked to hate

Or label "problematic." "Ziri, 8

½," he said. "First scene." He yawned and sank

Down on his futon. In his fauna tank,

A sleeping bonsai panther wagged its tail.

The mail had yet to beam down on the mail

Pad by the door.

               The smartpaint on his wall

Began to play Fellini's picture. (Small

Dead spots, where paint had chipped, stood out like stone

In rushing water.) Artists work alone,

The picture seemed to say. It was about

A film director, Guido, wracked with doubt

About his half-formed film, while all around

Distractions—mistress, wife, and actors—hound

Our hero. Hubert liked the lesson: men

Directing films have merely swapped out pen

For megaphone. They pick and place their herds

Of extras as a poet would his words—

Though *their* words, armed with legs, will often wander

Off.

     Fellini's man had paused to ponder

Life. His wife, it seemed, thought he'd outgrown her.

But Hubert liked that Guido was a loner

Floating like a god above the fray.

Of course, he knew that those who brood the way

Fellini's privileged male director does

Ignore the drones enabling them, the buzz
Of labour on the set. And yet he felt
The self behind each scene. The cult band Felt,
The poet Frost, Fellini—Hubert knew
Their work expressed their souls, which passed clean through
Our sieve-like theories. Souls were real, the art
They made the proof.
                                    The film had reached the part
Where Guido and his wife explore the set
That's been constructed for the film he's yet
To start: a giant spaceship's skeleton,
The sort of ship some blob of gelatin
With tendrils would attack. The science fiction
Of a simpler age. He loved this vision,
Hubert, of a future that would never
Happen now. He pictured it whenever
He imagined what tomorrow might
Be like. Fellini's spaceship, poised for flight,
Was dated now, a silly dream, but in
Its time, it gleamed. Likewise, a dorsal fin
Was *de rigueur* when navigating stars
In 1960s Jetsons bubble cars.
And in the novel *Neuromancer*, human
Beings—jacked in, wearing trodes—would zoom in
On vast tiers of data; outer space
Had been replaced by pre-Zuck "cyberspace,"
Which Hubert figured would've looked like *Tron*:
The ground a grid your avatar slid on.

The futures we prefer have long since passed.
Tomorrow is interred inside the past.

Hubert loved looking back. He'd waved off eye
Replacements; Hubert had a glasses guy
Who sourced assorted old-school gear for old
Souls and their skulls. His frames were bold,
As quaint as whalebone corsets, hunting foxes,
iPhones, and those primitive Xboxes
That weren't implanted but, instead, sat on
Your furniture. He loved the off-brand dawn
His window ran, recorded when the sun
Could still be seen. He loved such stuff as *Fun
House*, *Horses*, *Astral Weeks*, *The La's*, *Pet Sounds*,
Thomas Disch's essays, Ezra Pound's
Translations, Orson Welles as Harry Lime
(*The Third Man*), poetry that dares to rhyme,
The books of Paula Fox, the bass of Carol
Kaye, that moment when the poet Daryl
Hine compares some "love-disordered linen"
To "brackish water." Hubert longed for hymns in
Churches, first editions, and constraint.
He loved the room he rented in a quaint
Toronto house. He loved artisanal walks.
(He wouldn't teleport.) He thought Talk Talk's
Last record music's cloud-wreathed apex; Toto
Its nadir.
             On the mail pad, MOJO
Materialized. (The mail beamed in at night.)

"Pause." The wall became a black-and-white
Tintype: Fellini's hero's face in doubt.
(One eye, where paint had chipped, appeared burned out.)

Hubert watched his mag, like *Star Trek* sand,
Take shimmering shape, then touched it with a hand:
Still warm.
                          There was the standard MOJO mix
Of articles, reviews, and concert pics.
There also was an obit for Oasis;
The aging band had fused and perished, faces
Picassoed, moptops mixed—a teleporter
Mishap while on tour. One shrewd reporter,
Who'd glimpsed the Cubist mess, could not refrain
From wit: the band's two stars now shared one brain,
Which was ironic; Liam and Noel, rock gods
And warring brothers, spent their lives at odds.
But now their hearts, once split in two, were one
Big mashup of a muscle in a ton
Of flesh—the band's last huddle.
                                          Noel's song "Slide
Away" was playing; Hubert had subscribed
To MOJOplus, the upper-price-point version
Of the mag—and Hubert's main diversion
From the grind of grad school. MOJOplus,
On pixiepaper, was superfluous,
But awesome. If you tapped a tintype (what
His folks once called "a foto") it would strut
Or speak or turn into a talking head
Voice-overing some footage. If you read
About a song, the page might start to play
Its chords. That said, the reader had no say
In when concentric liquid ripples might
Begin to spread across the text, a white
And foamy head of Stella swallowing
The type; or when the letters, following

Their own discreet imperatives, might swarm
Like filings in magnetic fields to form
A BMW. A barnacle
Of kale might crawl across an article
And bloom into an ad for superfood.
Your MOJOplus could analyze your mood,
Decide you need more sleep, and push a pill
Designed for you alone—bespoke ZzzQuil.
On pixiepaper, type, no longer black
And fixed, could stretch, divide, curl up, go slack,
And vanish. Pics could puddle, spread, and blend,
Like Rorschach blots set loose.
                                            Towards the end
Of every MOJO was the "Buried Treasure"
Essay. This one-page feature took the measure
Of some minor work time had forgot
To, well, forget or scrub from human thought:
The sort of record that was out of print
Or went for hundreds when described as "mint."
And it was *this* page, in the June edition,
Hubert later likened to a vision.

* * *

The subject of the essay was the one
And only single by a band whose run
Had not been long (it lasted for six years)
But should've yielded more. What looked like tears
Began to streak the page; the beads that form
On sweating cans of Coke began to storm
The paper. Hubert shook the mag, which closed
The ad (though some ads couldn't be opposed
And ran full length). He turned back to the text

And read some more—and found himself perplexed.
The tintype of the band, when Hubert tapped
It, failed to move, as if the men were trapped
Inside. (The guy who manned the double bass,
He should've started plucking it, his face
unfreezing.) Was there video? A sample
Track? He read on, lest some lion trample
The text into a logo for a zoo
Or jungle travel package—read on through
In awe.
        They'd formed around 2007,
Three decades back, when Montréal was heaven,
And not the Crater. They'd struggled with their name,
Had gone by Lout, at one point, then Pale Flame,
Before they found the winner: Mountain Tea.
Hubert's favourite work of poetry!
James Gordon, MT's founder, had adored
The book.
        The band's debut, *The Dead*, had floored
Reviewers. Over reverbed brass and strummed
Guitar, as choral cowboy voices hummed
Spaghetti-Western-style, the singer read
A list of lost, neglected bands in dead-
Pan: "Felt" (pause), "Plush" (pause)—each pause punctuated
By piano chord. The choir abated,
Giving way to H.U. Hawks's bass,
A pulse that emphasized the empty space
It echoed in. Two vintage theremins
Began to moan. A ghost—George Harrison's?—
Possessed guitarist Louis Reid and made
Him play a riff a Beatle might've played,
A spectral solo that was mesmerizing,

Masterful, low strings now slowly rising,
Singer Dennis Byrne imploring—crying—
"Raise the dead!"
                        (Hubert kept on trying
The tintype. Nothing, not one note, would play.)

The B-side to the single, "Yesterday,"
Was not a cover of the Beatles hit,
But dared to spirit off the name and spit
On sacred ground. It started with "a one,
A two," and ended with a fired gun.
The sound was scratchy; they had used old field
Recording gear—like Harry Smith would wield
When mingling with less "modern" folk—to capture
Faraway, primeval sounds of rapture,
Carbonated with the hiss and pop
That means the past. A kind of horse's-clop,
Produced with legs chopped off a thoroughbred—
Or so the song's percussionist had led
The writer to enthuse—clip-clopped along,
While Gordon, singing just on this one song,
Described his lost beloved's smile. Reid,
Invoking punk rock, spewed a cloud of feed-
Back. Hawks supplied some bass notes on a Moog
To underscore the lost beloved's fugue
State. Byrne took mallets to a vibraphone.
A cello in slow-mo began to drone.
The MOJO writer, awestruck, judged this start
Not just a strong debut; this work was art.

But that was it. James Gordon's band put out
No more—and vanished. Only the devout,

Who'd bought *The Dead* on vinyl years before,
Had heard it. Mountain Tea's two songs were more
Or less a myth tied up in legal woes.
That's why the essay featured only prose;
The bots inside the paper grain could link
To nothing. So they stayed as still as ink.

2.

A postcard flew through Patti's field of vision,
Then paused, afloat: "Your piece in June edition
Of MOJO."

        "Flag for later," Patti mumbled.
The postcard, foxed and sepia-tinted, tumbled
Into her inbox, represented by
A folder in the corner of her eye.
She blinked two times — the folder disappeared —
And tried refocusing.

              On stage, a beard-
Embellished man in flannel and a toque
Was reading from a book — a stark rebuke
To those who'd swapped their birth eyes for a pair
Of smart ones; those who often seemed to stare
At you when, really, they were reading mail
Or Zwitter. True: the text could freeze and fail
To clear, which *could* leave lines of words imposed
Upon one's world. But mostly typetalk closed
When one desired. Mostly it was privileged
Assholes — artists, poets, profs — who pillaged
Bookstores, made a point of loving print,
And rolled their eyes at those obliged to squint
Because a postcard no one else could see

Was floating by. The world was undersea:
A billion private oceans (one per set
Of pupils) through which people trudged, beset
By flotsam.
                    Fuck it, Patti *liked* her notes
Uploaded to her eyes. She liked how motes
Swam through the reef of type. To each, she thought,
Her own. (Of course, she sometimes had to swat
Away unwanted spam, which circled like
A shark.)
                    But bearded dude, up at the mic,
Was too much. Post-Its bristled from his pages:
Notes which poets, when they take to stages,
Seem to need to mark the parts they want
To read. It's almost like they need to flaunt
Their hopelessness, thought Patti with a sigh.
She sipped her pint. She'd promised to stop by
Her best friend's launch, but hadn't counted on
An opening act: some bro critiquing brawn.

Tatt-sleeved poets sat around the room.
Candlelight ensured artisanal gloom.

Collection drones were circulating through
The bar and filming people's praise in lieu
Of cash donations. Floating by, a sphere
With single cyclops eye had paused to peer
At Patti. "Please say something nice," it said
Metallically, "about the bards who've read
Tonight. We post on ZuckTube's Hoot." She tried
To turn away. It orbited and eyed

Her with its lens, which shuttered once: a blink.
Patti paused. "I mean, they make you think?"

Up near the stage, up next, her friend was marking
Her book's pages. Bearded dude was barking
Something about his white male privilege.
These poets seemed to think it sacrilege
To rhyme or hold a beat. She double-blinked
Her inbox open and, half-crouching, slinked
Towards the door. The postcard, from a certain
"Hubert," began to load.
                                        A beaded curtain,
Each bead floating, parted on its own
Like bangs gone rogue. A neon sign—"ALONE
AGAIN," alluding to the song by Love—
Lit Patti as she stepped outside. A dove
With red eyes hung above the street. A Zuck
Maps drone. Of course, it would be just her luck
To be immortalized in Street View right
Outside a bar known for its "Poets Night."
She wore a Slits tee, jeans, and vintage blazer,
Which she'd slashed in places with a razor.

The postcard followed Patti's pupils—fluent
As it floated. But it went translucent
As she turned and squinted at a passing
Car. Her eyes relaxed. As if amassing
Molecules, the card firmed up again.
A line of cursive, by an unseen pen,
Unwound from left to right. She didn't want
To be a cynic. But a clever font

Was bad news. First-year English undergrads
Will fuck with defaults. So, too, old folks. Dads.

This "Hubert" loved her piece on Mountain Tea.
But hits about the book of poetry
Were all his searches found. The Zuck—the sum
Of human thought once called the "Web"—was mum
On Gordon's four-piece. Hubert couldn't find
A fan page, essay, zwiki—zilch. "The mind
The Zuck appears to make material,"
He wrote, "a mind that seems ethereal
Until, that is, computers intermingle,
Has drawn a blank. It can't recall a single
Thought of Mountain Tea." (She thought that last
Graf slightly purple.) "How then," Hubert asked,
"Does someone hear their songs?"
                                    Then Patti heard
Her friend's name called. Back in ALONE, a furred
Man, MC for the night, was reading press.

"Harper's books of poetry impress.
Her poems speak of witness, self, and loss."
A spotlight, when he shifted, slid across
His pelt. "Please welcome Harp!" He beat his paws.
The modest crowd erupted in applause
And overheated hoots, the sort reserved
For friends whose lack of fame, although deserved,
Still somehow *feels* unjust. (Fortune passes
Talent out to some, but never masses.)

Patti was a freelance music critic.
She knew the joke—what rhymes with parasitic?—
But still believed that any kind of writing
Could be art, and loved to read a biting
Essay. Critics ought to show some fangs,
She thought. They ought to be like Lester Bangs.
But Bangs's sharp reviews were contraband;
Like Kael and Disch, he'd long ago been banned
By Authors for a Safer World, whose mission
Was to snuff out snark in criticism,
Which they felt was harmful. Harsh reviews
Of works of art—reviews that left a bruise—
Could bring their wrath. Their membership remained
A mystery, their tactics unrestrained.
(They'd torched three men.) Their logo was a hoop
Of light. The lines of longitude that loop
An Earth have come unstuck and stand like bars
Before the globe. Behind this planet, stars—
Stylized dots—suggest that outer space
Itself is now a vacuum-sealed safe place.

So critics only wrote about the things
They loved. The rules were clear: an essay sings
Its object's praises or it's forced to fume,
Cast on kindling, purified by plume.
Few writers dared to file hatchet jobs;
Balaclavaed men were lashing snobs
To stakes. The final words of William Logan,

"These flames aren't hot enough," were now the slogan
For an underground society
Of US critics pledged to irony
And snark. Their pop-up pamphlet *Hatchet Job*
Would smother other websites like the Blob.
You'd visit *Slate* and find a single post—
"The Heti Books We Love to Hate the Most"—
On white, in Franklin Gothic Medium.
(The byline always used a pseudonym.)

The rumour was the critic Anthony Lane
Had started *Hatchet Job*. "We must refrain
From censoring ourselves," the critic wrote
To sympathetic writers, from a boat
That never docked. His words found Patti's eyes:
"We need your wit." She used to idolize
The older writer. Lane had even praised her
Prose once. Trolling, doxing—nothing phased her.

She took the gig—and took a hatchet to
The latest Taylor Swift, *My Feud with You*,
Then sent the piece to editor@hatchet-
Job.dark. The rules were clear: "Attach it
To a postcard. Please don't sign your name
Or reference loved ones. This is not a game.
Too many have already disappeared."

A few weeks later, Patti's piece appeared
And blotted out the homepage for *The Post*,
Its Franklin Gothic barnacling its host.
Harper's, *Slate*, *The New York Times*, *The Nation*—

Each one, fearful, signaled condemnation.
And Authors for a Safer World declared
The unknown critic should be very scared.

So Patti said, no more, that's it, I'm done.
But couldn't help but write another one.
And then another. Patti couldn't seem
To stop. She'd found a secret way to scream.

* * *

The pelt guy, eyeing Patti, felt like trouble.
She left soon after Harper read, then double-
Blinked. Five postcards spouted from her folder—
First, the newer ones, and then, the older—
Slowing down to spin before her face.
Alerts from Zuckgram. Zuckbook. "Fireplace,"
She said. A pixelated eight-bit flame,
Alluding to some vintage video game,
Consumed each card revolving round her head.

"Compose reply to Hubert," Patti said,
And as she walked and talked, a line of prose
Traversed her view like text on TV shows.
She whispered, "Send." A postcard formed a backdrop
And whisked the words away. She guessed a laptop
On the other end—there was no lapse
In style. Hubert used italics. Caps.

"How 'bout we chat tomorrow?" (Her suggestion.)
"Sounds great!" he wrote back. "*One* quick question:
How *did* you first discover Mountain Tea?—

The band, I mean. (I know the poetry.)"
They started trading postcards back and forth,
As Patti headed home, which was due north.

Her beat, she wrote, was music from the past
Deserving praise. The albums made to last.
The proven. Even then, what drew her love
Were often bands the world had not heard of,
Like Mountain Tea. She didn't even own
The vinyl for *The Dead*, their only known,
Impossible-to-source-or-hear release.
She'd stumbled on them through a piece
Of tech a year ago—an iPod shuffle.
A Craigslist bot was selling from a duffle
Bag of curios out on the street.
The iPod, on a chain, looked kinda neat
Repurposed as a charm. She hadn't thought
The antique thing would work, but when she got
It home and charged it up, an apple lit
The screen. What's more, it still contained a bit
Of sound: a playlist titled "Archive," by
The artist "Mountain Tea." She wondered why
The iPod wasn't wiped, but when she went
And played the songs, she knew the gods had meant
For her to hear them. (Patti often filed
On cult figures, those who were exiled
Or neglected.)
                    Mountain Tea, however,
Were so murky even *she* had never
Heard of them, this dry-ice-shrouded band.
It took some research just to understand
The contents of the list: two finished tracks,

The single's songs, and other scraps—a sax
Part (song-less, on its own) called "Horn Part (Rough),"
Whose notes seemed carved in stave but off the cuff
As well. Inspired.
                              Another scrap was called
"For Dennis Wilson." Patti was enthralled
By Wilson's solo work. He'd been the drummer
For The Beach Boys, distillate of summer
Days, the one who surfed, chased girls, and did
His best to hold the beat. He was pure id,
Swapped out at times for session pros. But when
He started writing songs, The Beach Boys, men
Resigned to hawk their hits, were stunned. They hadn't
Thought that Dennis (boyband manboy) had it
In him. His songs were dark, piano-driven
Products of a life that love had riven.
It sounded, Wilson's voice, unsanded: deep
And rough, the rasp of someone roused from sleep
And forced to sing his dreams. The mix would swell
With strings the way an eye will sometimes well
Up, gleam, and overflow. In time, he stopped
Recording. (Wilson's solo work had flopped.)
He drank a sea and drowned in '83.

"For Dennis Wilson," by this "Mountain Tea,"
Began with bass harmonicas, which sounded
Like the wheezing of a man confounded
By the knowledge of the art he *could*
Create if only inner demons would
Collaborate with better angels. (That's
A line she had been saving.) Then, like bats
In flight, the drums—run backward in the mix—

Flip-flapped from ear to ear. A pair of picks
Plucked out a mood. Low strings washed in, synthetic
Ones in lieu of bows. The track—ascetic,
Lacking vocals—clearly was a rough
Take. Had they stayed together long enough
To finish it, well look, I mean, who knows...
(This was the theme of much of Patti's prose.)

Another song that Mountain Tea had failed
To move beyond the demo phase still nailed
Itself to memory. (A fucking Beatle
Could've authored it.) Perhaps a beat still
Needed to be added. As it was,
Though, "Song"—a single voice, plus chainsaw buzz
Of faraway guitar—seemed fully formed.
Fault-free. (Of course, it could've been performed
But once, its only audience two spools
Of tape exchanging shapes.)
                                                    The rest were jewels
As well, jarred loose from settings you were forced
To fantasize about, which reinforced
A feeling something great had gone amiss.
These fragments, poems by Anonymous,
Were notes towards a work that never was.
Of course, the sound was poor and burred with fuzz.
What's more, the critic found she couldn't post
The tracks. The record label, Goat, had ghosted
Her requests. Turns out the label, based
In Montréal, had been destroyed—erased
By Crater. When she tried to post *The Dead*,
A barrister bot descended on the thread
And scrubbed it clean. (The label must've set

The bot up years before.) To date, she'd yet
To source a disc.

                No wonder no one seemed
To know this band—it was as if she'd dreamed
Them into being, Patti wrote to Hubert,
Walking down the street. Imagine Schubert-
Level genius, ambered in an iPod,
Found by chance. You gotta wonder why God
Let there be such noise when ears were wanting.
Even short-lived Schubert, briefly flaunting
Genius, flickered long enough to find
A modest cult to keep his sound in mind.
His followers had held their ground like wicks;
They'd held his torch while Schubert crossed the Styx.
(A vacuum is a firebrand's great terror.)
"Here music has buried a treasure, but even fairer
Hopes," his gravestone said, as if it stocked
A dream to be exhumed.

* * *

                As Patti walked,
She typetalked cards to Harper ("Harper, wow,
Great job tonight"), her mother ("Mom, not now,
Okay? Let's talk on Tues"), her copyeditor
(A bot she loathed; whenever Patti fed it her
Latest draft, the program chirped, no matter
What, "Good start!", then duly left its splatter:
Blood-red edits), Hubert (bit intense),
And others. All around the air was dense
With private, floating type, as some dictated
Postcards, while others blinked and read. She hated
All these men and women shuffling slow

As zombies, lost in typetalk, even though
She was the same.

A haggard man lurched by
And batted at the air. He caught her eye—
His face afraid—but Patti looked away.
A swarm of unseen zweets had found their prey;
An in-eye mob was on him.

Cars sped past.
Aspiring writers—at their laptops, glassed
And framed by Starbucks windows—tried and failed
To work on memoirs, having been derailed
By flying postcards.

Patti felt a piece
Of paper in her pocket, with a crease
That wouldn't smooth itself: the dumbprint flyer
For her best friend's reading. These were dire
Times. Plus, it was sad to throw out tree-
Based paper stock. But Patti saw the Z-
Stamped chute—a sidewalk periscope—and balled
The flyer up. This sort of thing appalled
Her ex, an activist who'd make a face
When Patti threw things into outer space.
(The Z-Chute teleported waste off-planet,
Into the exosphere. He'd worked to ban it;
So-called "exostuff" had helped create
The Cloud, a fact subjected to debate
By right-wing pundits.)

Patti reached her port,
A vintage phone booth, minus phone: the sort
Of thing that knowing city dwellers loved.
(They also loved when metal hands were gloved
With calloused skin; when denim was distressed;

When bots, their plastic wet with gleam, were dressed
In dented tin to look like '50s droids;
When clunky cameras issued Polaroids
Like tongues; or when a table's natural edge
Had not been planed away. They loved to dredge
The past, provided modern comforts were
In place. Even Post-Men, those with fur
Implanted, tended to prefer a hide
That was real skin but also modified
In lab, ensuring hypoallergenic
Properties. In short, they loved authentic,
Rustic things, but only if the rust
Was Zuckgram-worthy: gold disguised as crust.)

Patti stepped inside the booth, which read
Her eyes for passport pin. She yawned and said,
"Toronto, Parkdale." Something clicked. The phone-
Booth's windows went opaque. A kind of drone
Had started up. Her skin began to feel
As if its molecules, now loose, were peeling
Off; as if her body, carbonated,
Were fizzing at its edges. Patti hated
How it felt, but then she blinked and there
She was: no longer in New Brooklyn, where
The reading was, but now—and in the space
Of seconds—in Toronto, face to face
With *her* paned face, both eyes raccooned with black
(After Gaye Advert: punk girl from way back).
The face was smudgy, scuffed, and fingerprinted.

But then the booth's graffitied panes un-tinted;
The face went out. A crowd streamed past the port

Where Zuber's bots had quickly worked to sort
Out Patti's molecules.

                            "So *we're* like Schubert's
Coterie," a postcard noted; Hubert's
Reply had had to wait for Patti's eyes
To coalesce.

                    She left the booth. Two guys,
Both drunk, said something to her. Hubert's "*we're*"
She'd leave for now; she figured she should steer
Him back to tangibles. "How 'bout I send
A copy of the iPod?" (That'll end
The thread, she figured.)

                                "Sure, that's awesome! Glad
To have it!" Pause. But how, he wondered, *had*
She learned enough about MT to write
Her piece? How could a band avoid the light
This long? Some bands are minor, but you've heard
Of them at least, or there's a trail a nerd
Can follow: zines, recordings, clippings, baseless
Rumour. Even Thomas Pynchon, faceless
Hermit, had put out books that people bought.
(Like whistleblowers rendered as a blot,
Or faces scrambled into pixel splatter,
He could *speak*.) But Mountain Tea, dark matter,
Had left nothing.

                        "Well," she wrote, "there's *some*
Stuff." Patti had found articles in dumb-
Print sources: codex books and bot-less screens.
(Read: paper.) Local music magazines
Reviewed *The Dead* when it came out. The Zuck
Does not remember them, but with some luck,

She found old copies in used bookstores on
The edge of Montréal. "Of course, they're gone,
These indie publications." Of course, he knew
What her "of course" implied; the Crater threw
A constant shadow.

                 There'd been a couple brief
Reviews. "This band," said one, "restores belief."
But some struck dark notes. One piece said James Gordon,
Who had led the group, had been its warden.
Impossible to please, he often burned
The tape that held their brilliant takes. (She turned
A corner. Nearly home.) He *had* okayed
The Dead—but only if the thing was made.
No MP3s, insisted Gordon. Vinyl.
He did one interview, his first and final.
He quoted Lawrence, cryptic leader of
The cult band Felt: the people who'll love
The Mountain—true fans won't say, "Mountain Tea"—
Have yet to be delivered, yet to be
Conceived! (As Patti typetalked, one hand rifled
For her keys.)

            But hadn't Gordon stifled
Mountain Tea, his interviewer wondered.
Gordon, tough perfectionist, had sundered
Ties, or so it seemed, with everyone
He'd ever worked with, even pulling guns,
Phil Spector-style, on his bandmates. Gordon
Laughed this off. Sure, I've been called a warden,
Quote unquote. Ridiculous. Was Byron
A brute for wanting ink to work? (A siren
Was approaching Patti.) Is it wrong

To want your band to execute a song
Exactly as it plays between your ears?
Remember Frost: no tears for writers, no tears
For readers.
                        Patti stopped. A fire alarm
Was going off. Ahead, she saw an arm
Of smoke, dark grey and muscled, rooting through
Her building—through her floor. (The sky it grew
From like a god personifying greed
And blindly grasping round.) The siren she'd
Been hearing dopplered by. A bright red, skull-
Faced fire engine. Its entire hull
Was blinking on and off, its pixieiron
Pulsing to the rhythm of the siren.
Bots sat in the skull, whose portholes, sockets,
Gave the engine eyes. (Two mounted rockets
Spewed twin vapour trails.) Outside her building,
Several other engines, parked, were gilding
Bushes, trees, and cars a throbbing red.

"I gotta go." She double-blinked the thread
Away and ran toward the blazing light.

A scroll flew into Patti's line of sight.
She batted at it, but the scroll kept pace
And, as she sprinted, got up in her face
And, like a shade tugged by a ghost, unfurled
Itself—"from Authors for a Safer World"—
Its parchment rippling as it tried to match
Her speed, the wind effect a clever patch
Of code. She blinked and blinked. It wouldn't close.
The scroll unwound a few more lines of prose:

"We know about your *Hatchet Job* reviews.
And yes, we are the ones who lit the fuse."

One fire engine looked like it was bawling;
Bots, their skin a creamy white, were crawling
From its portholes. Patti, running, saw
One plug an arm into a hydrant, draw
Away to face the blaze—the creamy plastic
Limb, attached, extending like elastic—
And, saluting, raise its other arm,
The low-rise building screaming its alarm.
No matter where she looked, the postcard stayed
In view. "Fireplace!" It wouldn't fade.

The bot's arm tapered to a handless snout.
It sputtered into life: a waterspout.

Only later, after paramedics
Had calmed her down—and only after FedEx,
Who made her inbox, had rebooted each
Of Patti's eyes, the victims of a breach,
A pupil hacking—was the scroll, which faced
Her panicked face 'til 5 a.m., erased.

3.

Gibson was typing in the dark café,
A room just off the entrance to Swann's Way,
Roppongi's finest bookshop. Smartbooks lined
The walls and mimicked what was on your mind.
Picture Pynchon's *V.*, and *V.*'s dust jacket
Re-skinned the nearest volume. If you hacked it,
Swann's Way's network, you could make the walls,
Each spine a pixel, spell out "Suck my balls,"
As someone did once. Mostly, though, the shelves
Were tame. They shifted slightly as if elves
Were making small adjustments to the room.

But Gibson, wincing, couldn't help assume
That other customers at nearby tables
Had middlebrows when books like *Aesop's Fables*
Were wiped and swapped for novels like *The English
Patient*. So he tended to extinguish
Other people's thought crimes once they'd left.
He'd pan his eyes, and books of wit and heft
Would primer over Eggers and Ayn Rand.
(He'd even summon books that had been banned.)
He looked like someone, forty, meditating,

When, in fact, his hater mind was hating.
Gibson found he had to fix at least a
Dozen crimes a day. A bot-barista
Stood behind the counter, filling mugs.
A dropped or shattered mug meant network bugs.

You could buy real books in the shop itself;
The smartbooks, scanning minds, were shelf
Décor, each one the same sad width. Thus *War
And Peace* looked oddly thin, *The Art of War*
A bit too thick. You couldn't really fool
Devoted readers. Still, the tech was cool.
And if you *had* imagined something thin—
A *Tender Buttons*, say—the font size in
The book would automatically increase
To fill the page count. Picture *War and Peace*,
However, and the type would shrink to mite-
Sized specks, too miniscule for human sight.

From time to time, a tourist would show up,
Remove her backpack, count out yen. A cup
Of something now in hand, she'd point her face
At several shelves and squint. The spines would race
Like panels on a mainframe changing colour,
Some spines lighting up or getting duller
As the tourist's favourite books displaced
Poor Gibson's picks, as other tastes refaced
The walls, as *Twilight* blotted *Hardy Boys.*

It was, for Gibson, one of life's great joys
To take a sip of tea and then envision

Mountain Tea, the Véhicule edition.
The volume's sky-blue spine would start to tile
Over nearby shelves. A work of style—
From back when Canada was void of verse,
As if its poets, victims of a curse,
Had been condemned to mediocrity—
Van Toorn's great book was more than poetry;
Some felt it was the rock band Mountain Tea's
Rosetta Stone.   But there were other keys
Preferred by other camps and subject to
Intense debate among the thousands who
Signed in to *Gordian Knot*, the bustling chat
Salon. Some felt that Gibson was a flat-
Earth theorist focused too much on a weird
Coincidence. These "Jamesians" revered
James Gordon as Auteur, the only source
Of meaning *and* The Mountain's driving force.
The rock band and the poems merely shared
A name—or so the Jamesians declared.

Gibson, "Van Toornian" at heart, believed
The Jamesians, who prized intent, deceived
Themselves. To know the band you had to look
To *Mountain Tea*—the great Van Toorn's lost book.
You had to scrutinize The Mountain's roots:
Allusions, predecessors, and disputes
With other works of art. Like Northrop Frye,
The true Van Toornian would need to try,

With gentle tugs, the references that bind
The poet's masterpiece to Gordon's mind.

Gibson's fingers worked the laptop keys.
His mind had filled the shelves with *Mountain Teas*.

He was the founder of the *Knot* and kept
The peace among its warring camps. He slept
Three hours on a good night, half an eye
On threads. His bedroom ceiling was a sky,
Its cloudless pixiepaint a field of stars.
When Gibson couldn't sleep, small avatars
Appeared down one side of the ceiling, posts
Beside each one. (His pallid face, a ghost's,
Would glow all night; the homepage was a night-
Light.) Gibson read the posts, but liked to write
Replies from Swann's Way, where he spent his days.
He'd sit within the bot-barista's gaze
And nurse a tea.
                    He'd been debating one
Of *Gordian Knot*'s top users, Set to Donne,
An orthodox Van Toornian, who clicked
With Gibson even though he often picked
At Gibson's scansion. Set to Donne, who swore
He had Van Toorn by heart, possessed a store
Of verse so vast he could live in a cage
For years, deprived of print, and simply page
Through all the poems printed on the tissue
Of his brain. That night, he'd taken issue

With a reading of a line from *Mountain*
Tea—whose rhythm seemed to match the count in
At the start of "Yesterday"—and taken
Tweezers to it, arguing with graven
Certainty that Gibson had misread
The meter. This had mostly cleared the thread.

None of them, of course, had heard a note.
Their love was based on words a woman wrote.

Gibson brought a hand up to his face
And rubbed his eyes, his glasses making space,
The armless lenses floating to the side.
(They sensed his movements, used them as a guide.)
He dropped the hand; the lenses judged it safe
To float back over. They were Anti-Chafe,
His Ray-Bans, but he couldn't help but flinch
As each lens flew back into place—an inch
Away from eyeball—using Gibson's brow
As baseline.
                              Gibson looked outside. A scow
Put down and let out several girls with bright
Blue pelts. The scow ascended out of sight.

He sipped his tea. A swan was gliding round
The mug's smooth surface, calm, without a sound.
Sometimes the mug displayed a madeleine,
Which gently turned in space. (It soon began
To shorten and, through unseen bites, reduced
To crumbs, which swarmed to form the face of Proust.
In time, the face resumed the biscuit's clam

Shape.) Someone's think-piece on an anagram
Of "Mountain Tea" was stirring up the *Knot*.

Gibson closed the site. He paused. Then brought
A message up. A boy's face filled the screen.

"Daddy, are you coming home soon?" Green
Eyes. Blonde hair.
                        "I'll be there real soon," he said.

A woman's voice: "Tell Dad to pick up bread."
Behind the boy, a pair of legs passed by.

He closed the message. Movement caught his eye.
He glimpsed the letter "G," spelled out in white-
Spined books across the room. Then like a light,
The "G" went out.
                        His laptop made a beep.
A postcard. Hayes. Who never seemed to sleep.

"Gibson, are you sitting down?" it said.
"I think I've found a copy of *The Dead*."

* * *

He pushed clean through the Hilton's entryway.
The liquid window stretched as if to stay
Attached to Gibson—then snapped back in place
And rippled like the surface of a lace-
Thin pond stood on its side. He heard some wails;
A pride of Post-Men filled the lobby, tails
Erect and brushing passersby in dare:

A drunken tour group. He tried not to stare.

He wore a side bag and a multi-pocket
Military shirt. He'd plugged the socket
Behind his ear—a disused, hair-fringed hobby
Port—with flesh-pink spirit gum.

                              The lobby
Was bustling. Gibson spotted Hayes beside
A fountain. Hayes had cut the pride a wide
Swath, and was staring at some unseen feed.
He hadn't shaved. His coat was dark-grey tweed.

Some folks had sworn off smarteyes. Some had had
Their fleshtech taken out. The fading fad
Had left its scars. You sometimes saw a bruise
Or bandage; such signs signalled, like tattoos,
A youthful folly. Gibson used to game
In-skull. His gaping neck hole was his shame.
But now, he didn't trust his cells to Zuber
Booths, preferring scows. A little super-
Stitious, but he didn't like to gamble.
This growing trend—avoiding atom scramble—
Was also big with movie stars, who taxied
For their health. (It was like taking flaxseed.)

Gibson caught Hayes's eyes; Hayes shook his head.
"The motherfucker got here just ahead
Of us," said Hayes. "Gone up already." Jazz
Was playing in the lobby.

                              "Course he has,"
Said Gibson, trying not to sound defeated.
The man in question, Edmund H, had cheated

Time and space before.
                    They took the lift
Up to the eighth. (They watched the numbers shift,
In silence.) Someone with an earpiece stood
Outside the room and waved them in.
                                    "We could
Just leave, you know," said Hayes. "Not give the guy
The satisfaction. Fucker's made the buy
By now."
            But Gibson, saying nothing, brushed
Past Mr. Earpiece. Edmund H had crushed
Their hopes before, but maybe they could steal
A glimpse of it, confirm the disc was real,
If out of reach.
                Inside the tiny space
Stood Edmund H, who kept his lower face
Behind a surgical mask and wore a light-
Grey suit; and facing him, a bot in white
Capris and fitted tee, whose muscled limbs
Were tan and glossy like a mannequin's.
Its feet wore orange slides. Its head was head-
Shaped glass: an oval planed of bumps. It said,
"Hey, Hayes." The seller's face revolved inside
The glass to face them, features warped, applied
Across a globe and stretched. (The rigid neck
Declined to swivel, being old-school tech;
The pixelated kisser slid around
The glass with fish-bowl physics.) On the ground,
The slides remained in place. The muscled torso
Still faced H.
                "You have to let us borrow
That," said Gibson, nodding at the disc

That Edmund H was holding.

                                    "Too much risk,"
Said H, who duly slid the sleeve inside
A bag.

            "I'm sorry," said the bot. "I tried
To wait." The seller's face had frozen on
A pained expression; Wi-Fi overdrawn,
The bot was stationary. Seconds passed.
The head-shaped bulb went out. The darkened glass
Reflected Gibson's face: the prematurely
Silver hair, the tired eyes that surely
Needed closing. Sleep.

                            Hayes had made
This contact months ago. The seller stayed
At home, in Greece, and sold his wares by bot.
That day, he'd messaged Hayes, who served the *Knot*,
But must've messaged Edmund, too.

                                        Unphased,
Gibson turned to Hayes. "I think we've raised
Twelve K?" Hayes nodded. Gibson, turning back
To H, said, "*Twelve* K. Just to rip two tracks."

But H zipped up the bag and shook his head.
This was the seventh copy of *The Dead*
That H had outbid Hayes and Gibson for.

H pushed between them, heading for the door.
"Let's go," they heard him say to Earpiece Guy.

The seller's bot lurched back to life. An eye
In close-up, blinking, had eclipsed the egg-
Smooth glass: a zoom-in glitch. The bot's right leg

Was twitching. "Tried," the seller said. "I tried,
I tried..." It almost sounded like "I lied."

* * *

The Ur-text for the cult of Mountain Tea,
The scripture from which fans drew energy,
Was ten years old. This document, a piece
In MOJO, proved to be a tragic tease.
A few days after it appeared, a fire
Struck the author's home. (She'd drawn the ire
Of a terror group for other stuff
She'd dared to publish.) No one meant to snuff
Out Mountain Tea, of course. But arson's sloppy.
The fire swallowed up the one known copy
Of "The Dead," plus B-side, trapped inside
An iPod. That fact hurt. The true fan died
A bit inside—as if the iPod were
Well, *their* tomb, too—but soon came to prefer
This fate; they still had MOJO's piece to fuel
Their dreams. They also coveted a cruel
Footnote: just after watching fire swallow
Up her place, the writer, like a hollow
Plot point in detective fiction, vanished.
Had some goddess of lacunae banished
Both the music *and* the human ears
That dared to hear it?
                              Several quiet years
Went by. In 2041, a man
Named "SchubertMinusSc" put a scan
He'd saved (a transcript of a dialogue
He'd had with MOJO's writer) on his zlog.
It mentioned scraps, an interview, reviews—

And MOJO's writer soon became a muse.
In fact, her typetalk only gained in stature.
The words she'd left behind ignited rapture
In some fanboys' minds. They'd seemed like song
The first time Gibson read them. Short and long
Beats. Verse.
        He taught a CanLit course at U
Of Tokyo, a contract gig he knew
Was shaky. So he founded *Gordian Knot*,
Where other desperate fans could post a thought
About this music they could only think
About. The chat salon began to link
The Mountain's diehards *and* earn Gibson just
Enough to pay his bills and hire a rusted
Scow to get around. (He liked to boast
The sky was his.)
        Some Knotters liked to post
Fan fiction. Argue. Someone called, "m(a)nFiction,"
Pictured Mountain Tea—and this caused friction
When she posted—as a female band.
(She set her stories in a world she'd planned
And plotted out with care. She'd even picked
Out names for rival rock bands; she was strict
About world building.) Gibson had his own
Fan project, *Dreaming Mountain Tea*, a tome
About a counterfactual Mountain Tea
That put out four LPs—a history
In rhyming couplets. Many Knotters spent
Their time discussing what the poems meant—
The poems of Van Toorn. The focus on
James Gordon's vanished band had come to spawn
Tangential interest in the poet's book.

(The thing was out of print, but if you shook
The Zuck, you'd find one.)
                    It was hard to keep
The *Knot* clean; pop-up pamphlets, which were cheap
To make, would hijack it from time to time.
An alt-right pamphlet, like a coat of slime,
Would cover up the posts. Conspiracy
And hate, which kept on gaining currency,
Would wipe away whole pages. Gibson, though,
Kept backups of the *Knot*. And when the snow-
White branding of the pamphlet for a Nazi
Group, The Ivory Troop, stormed in, a fancy
Keyboard move by Gibson sicced a bot
Upon the Troop's invasive code. The *Knot*
Would reappear, its branding's soft chartreuse
A kind of comfort.
                    Edmund H would use
The *Knot* from time to time. His tone was flat;
He rarely ever deigned to joke or chat.
A businessman, he mostly seized on rumour—
Vinyl sightings, say. His sense of humour
Was as stony as the face his moon-
White mask eclipsed. (He even had a goon.)
So when a seller posted that he'd found
A copy of *The Dead* with perfect sound
And zero scratches, Edmund—name a nod
To Edmund Hillary, the first non-god
To clamber to the top of Everest—
Outbid the *Knot*. He said he'd never rest
Until he owned a copy of *The Dead*—
But that he'd share it with the world. Then fled.
Refused DMs.

In fact, his surname was
Higashi. (First name: Eiichi.) Onzuck buzz
Put Edmund's net worth at ten billion Zuck-
Coins, give or take. He sometimes rocked a ruck-
Sack, quoting gear a mountaineer might wear.
He paid for *human* hands to cut his hair
And had a private, pricey Zuber stream—
No booth required. This meant he could beam
Down anywhere and snatch collectibles
From rivals. He was unrespectable
To some, but Gibson couldn't help admire
Someone else defined by his desire.

(Even Edmund's fountain pen was modelled
On the mountaineer's. An object swaddled
In its own mythology, it peeked
At times from Edmund's shirt and often piqued
The interest of a certain breed of Knotter.
Made of parts skilled hands had had to solder—
Parts recovered from the pens of dead
Victorians—the pen had spawned a thread
Still drawing comments.)
                              Two months after he'd
Secured that first disc—which he knew he'd need
To broadcast—Edmund re-emerged and posted
Video of a lavish masque he'd hosted
One night on his pristine private boat
In Tokyo Bay. A bonsai mountain goat
Stood on one shoulder as H faced the camera,
Monologuing on his courage, stamina,
Strength, and grit. He paused to dab a tear.
(The bonsai goat was nibbling at his ear.)

That's when the camera panned and came to rest
Upon a pedestal. It did its best
To focus; drunken men lurched in and out
Of shot, their faces masked—a piggish snout
On one, a sheep's head on another. Then,
The shot resolved. And all the onzuck men
And women at their screens were face to face
With, yup, the single in a thick glass case.

In time, the *Knot* would prize these video stills.
True fans would learn to look past Edmund's swills
Of wine—past background revelry—and study
The sleeve. But *that* night, those onzuck vowed bloody
Murder when H vowed he wouldn't play
Or make a copy of the disc. "The day
May come," he said, "but first *another* copy
Must be found." A light-brown rose with floppy
Petals, his corsage, appeared to share
Its DNA with something like a hare
And curled away from Edmund's nibbling goat.
The camera shook as water rocked the boat.

* * *

"You gonna be okay tonight?" said Hayes.
  They stood outside the Hilton.
                                  Gibson's gaze
Was tilted upward at the grid of head-
Lights in the sky. It looked like stars had fled
Their constellations for a life of grid-
Lock over Tokyo. The headlights slid,
Stopped dead, lurched forward. Gibson waved a hand;
A star dropped from the grid, a thinning strand

Of smoke in tow. Exhaust. The scow put down
Beside the two men.
                              "Gibs?" said Hayes. A crown
Of light afloat above the scow said, "Royal
Cabs." The scow was bobbing on a coil
Of air. It was a car sans body—just
An undercarriage, flaking into rust
And bearing bench seats, with a driver at her
Wheel. The thing was basically a platter,
Domed with liquid glass (the sort of bubble
Cake waits under), which the wind would ruffle.
Fuel tanks bulged beneath—as sleek and round
As insect parts—a few feet off the ground.

"I'm fine, I swear," said Gibson, getting in.
He looked up at his friend. He forced a grin.
Another reclaimed copy of *The Dead*
Would go unplayed, its liner notes unread.
Edmund's other six were locked up tight.

The scow took off. The sky was dark with light
Pollution: holo ads that came out nightly.
Across Shibuya's rooftops, stepping lightly,
Dancers, big as buildings, executed
Grand jetés, their holographic, fluted
Hemlines lifting like pavilions plucked
By wind. Gigantic manga lovers fucked
Above a love hotel, discarded socks
Afloat like clouds. The bay was on the rocks,
The water filled with crate-sized cubes of ice:
An ad for Nikka Whisky. Bowls of rice,
Uprooted amphitheaters, drifted over

Tsukiji. The scow zipped past the holos, hover
Trucks, and traffic lights—free-floating spheres
Of yellow, red, and green, which hung like tears
Arrested in midair.
                              "Turn left up here,"
Said Gibson to the driver's head: a clear
Bulb, like the seller's bot's. This one contained
An older Japanese man's face, engrained
With many wrinkles.
                              Gibson loved to be
In motion: in a hired scow or free
To move on foot. He loved the 2-D picture
Solaris and its city of the future:
Tokyo in 1972.
(There was no budget; Tokyo would do.)
Specifically, he loved the highway scene,
In which the concrete skyline on the screen,
Though real, still somehow passes for a place
That's yet to come. (The lesson: we must face
The fact the future's here.) And in the scow,
Lights streaking by, he felt his here and now
Begin to smear. He felt like he was out
Of time and skimming over it: a trout
Against a river's current.
                              Gibson counted
Out his fare. He pictured singles, mounted
Under glass and dusted by a man-
Sized bot. (Outside, a huge Sapporo can
Passed by the scow: a granary unmoored
By gale-force gusting.) Edmund H abhorred
The thought of wearing down his vinyl so
Much that he couldn't let his issues go

And simply play the discs. The goal of finding
Worn-out copies, which he wouldn't mind
Degrading, had consumed him. This meant not
A single soul had heard his discs; the *Knot*
Continued searching. Dreaming.

                       "That roof there
Is good," said Gibson, pointing at a square
Of lights: a capsule hotel's landing pad.
(Its pixieasphalt cycled through an ad
For room rates.) Gibson's scow began its plunge,
Straight through a sea blob—holo cleaning sponge—
And landed.

            A lift took Gibson to his floor:
A long and light-beige tunnel, smooth but for
A grid of white lines, slightly raised, which lined
The tube. (You could walk up its walls and find
Yourself inverted.) Gibson walked and found
His square. He thumbed a pocket fob. The ground
Below turned viscous. Gibson sank (or rose)
Into his capsule. Nothing stained his clothes;
The liquid plastic slid indifferently
Across, amoeba-like. Dizzily—
The gravity had flipped—he found himself
Thumped back-first on a bed. Beside, a shelf
Held books, one cup, a kettle. Overhead,
The plastic sealed.

                He sat up on the bed,
De-shouldered bag, kicked off his shoes, and, feeling
Blindly, turned the kettle on. The ceiling—
Having hardened, inches from his skull—
Displayed the *Knot* across its curving hull;
The capsule's pixiepaint was set to run

His laptop when he entered. Set to Donne
Had now signed off. (He lived in Tokyo
As well.) A Knotter based in Buffalo
Was up and posting. Gibson poured his tea.
The *Knot*, which left him dappled, was a tree
Disclosing sunlight.

                    Sometimes Gibson fought
The urge and won. But not today. He brought
The message up again.

                    "Daddy, are
You coming home soon?" Each green eye a star
Upon the capsule's ceiling.

                       "I'll be there
Real soon," he said again. (But it was rare
For him to watch it twice.)

                    The woman said—
She always said—"Tell Dad to pick up bread."
Behind the boy, the pair of legs passed by
As always.

            Sometimes Gibson wondered why
He hadn't asked the boy to tilt the screen
Up at the woman, who would stay unseen
Forever now. But how was he to know
That in the izakaya just below
Their small two-bedroom, flames were feeding on
An apron. Soon, the apron would be gone.
The flames would leap and spread and swallow up
His wife and son. He sipped his fuming cup
Of tea. "Please close recording."

                      Gibson learned
About The Mountain—and the iPod, burned
Up in a fire of its own—a few

Months later. Found the seminal review
In MOJO. That was when he formed the *Knot*,
Where desperate men like him could post a thought.

* * *

A few days later, working in Swann's Way,
He looked up. All the smartbooks had gone grey.
"A network glitch," explained the bot-barista.

Earlier, m(a)nFiction had unleashed a
Well-deserved shit storm on Set to Donne,
Who'd posted that The Mountain needed nun-
Like devotees to model piousness.
The chat salon had since turned riotous
As Pattis—*Gordian Knot*'s more feminist
Subscribers—piled on. A specialist
In semiotics had begun a thread
On symbols in the sleeve art for *The Dead*.
(Her source texts were the videos that Edmund
Posted after every purchase: seven
To date, revealing glimpses of the sleeve.)
And Hayes was off pursuing leads. He'd leave
A post from time to time; he had a column,
Hayes's Gaze, a fun if somewhat solemn
Zlog for *Gordian Knot*, about his quest
For copies of *The Dead*. A "Hashtag Blessed,"
Whose handle was ironic, had put up
Some drawings of The Mountain.
                                                    "One more cup
Of tea," said Gibson to the bot. Swann's Way
Was almost empty.
                              Suddenly, the grey

Spines all lit up. The shelves turned solid white.
Then, one by one, as if an unseen sprite
Were tapping spines, specific books turned blue.
The walls were spelling words. "GEOFF GIBSON, YOU
AND I SHOULD MEET. MY NAME IS HAL U. HAWKS.
I PLAYED IN MOUNTAIN TEA." The books, like blocks,
Continued stacking up. "WE MUST CHAT FURTHER."
A final spine stayed blinking, like a cursor.

4.

From *Twilight of The Mountain*, by m(a)nFiction.
A Romance. Book the Fourth.

                              The crucifixion
Captivated Janey Gordon all
Through senior year. Above her bed, the wall
Collaged assorted Christs on crosses, clipped
From pixiepaper. One Christ, being whipped,
Stared down at Janey from her bedroom ceiling,
Where more prints and clippings, corners peeling,
Were taped. (The sound was off, his mouth an "O"
As armoured Roman soldiers dealt the blow
By blow.) She liked an off-brand Christ: Gauguin's,
Say. Klimt's. She felt the cover of her band's
LP would need a Son of God, head tilted,
T-squared out. (Projected title: *Jilted
Nun*—though *Roman Holiday* was in
Play, too.)
                "I'm Good (I Want to Keep My Sin),"
Their set list's leadoff track, was emblematic
Of their sound: guitars like automatic
Fire; slurred-out slogans in affected
Cockney accent; words like "fuck" ejected
Gob-like; total playing time of two-

Point-five-ish minutes. ("Jesus was a Jew,
You Nazi You" came next.)
                              Louise, guitarist,
Stared at Converse when she played, as artists
Should, her hair a wall that cordoned off
Her face. Denise, the singer, liked to cough
Her lyrics out. Four dino spines, green spikes,
Went round her head. (A tattoo, heads on pikes,
Went round her neck, a picket fence of ink.
The tattoo was supposed to make you think,
She liked to say.) The drummer was a dude
Named Edward. Shirtless, pale, he liked to brood
And rarely smiled. Hailey Hawks, on bass,
Was bald.
                      They had a huge rehearsal space—
A ballroom, candlelit—in Janey's ancient
Mansion. (Her folks were dead. A kindly, patient
Nanny bot had raised her from the age
Of four.) The band was set up on the stage
And aimed their songs at sheet-draped furniture.
They played to ghosts, their works of art too pure
For human ears.
                          The bot, on bulbous wheels,
Approached with snacks. The band emitted squeals
Of joy: "It's Alma!" Janey loved her bot,
But reading Wolf had left a mark: the thought
That Alma's wheels, designed to mimic hips,
Were sexist.
                      "Mis-tress Jane," it said, with blips
And bloops. "Your med-i-cine." The girls descended
On the snacks. "De-nise, your hawk is splen-did,"
It declared, while handing Janey pills,

Each one dark crimson. (Edward, doing fills,
Stayed seated at his drum kit, staring dead
Ahead.)
                    Janey took the pills and said,
"Let's go again." Their high school dance—The Ghostly
Sock Hop—was next week. But they were mostly
Ready.
            Alma wheeled around and left.
Hailey cocked her axe and played a deft
And fluid bassline. Edward fell in line
Behind her. Janey watched them play, Ed's fine
Black hair cascading down his shirtless back.
His skin was chalk. The ballroom's curtains, black,
Were drawn. He grinned at Hailey; she grinned, too.
They shared a groove.
                        That evening, Janey flew
Above the mansion's grounds, as thoughts of Edward
Circled. Her dress was wind-filled. Banking westward,
She glimpsed the flutter-flicker of a campfire,
The sort of forest light that draws a vampire.

But not tonight. She plunged toward the mansion—
She occupied the half-complete expansion,
Started when her mum and dad were still
Alive—flew in across the windowsill,
And squatted on the ceiling. A chandelier—
A froth of light and glass, composed of tear-
Shaped crystal—seemed to stand upon its chain,
The links stretched taut. She crawled across the plain
Of concert posters, prints, and Munch's *Screams*.
She yawned, curled up, and sank into her dreams...

* * *

From *Hayes's Gaze: A Zlog*. May 23rd,
2047.

      Last night, this bird
Alighted on my narrow balcony;
The neighbour's boy was at his falconry
Again. I watched it as I laced my shoes,
Inside. Above, the *Knot*'s homepage, chartreuse,
Looked like a window to a forest world.
About a dozen unread postcards swirled
Around, as well: small scraps of paper borne
By flying Gundams, each scrap ragged, torn
From binding. (This is how I need to see
My mail.) The bird, a falcon, seemed to me
A sign, though. So I waved away the ring
Of mail and tried to focus on the thing
Itself. I left the *Knot* afloat; one day,
I'll close it. Smiley face.

                    The bird was gray
And crisscrossed with a grid of blood-red lines.
(Its plumage, as it grew, displayed designs
Preset by hobbyists.) The grid was sort
Of like the plain of play on which a sport
Unfolds in old computer games: a stark
And geometric net of red the dark
Defines. (I'm trying really hard these days
To be more present and to train my gaze
On life. I'm reading Locke. I look at art.)

I bought my dinner at the Family Mart
I sleep above: my standard katsu sando.
Ate on foot and crossed Omotesando.

Found the disused Zuber booth I like
To use for US trips. Its glass is spiked,
But once it senses me, the spikes retract.
Several years ago, I sorta hacked
It. Now the booth is cool with what I bring
Inside: my sharp-resistant Kevlar thing—
A grid-like colony of bots that's spun
Itself around my muscles—and my gun
Wand, for protection. Winky smiley face.
I've taught the booth to beam me up through space,
Beneath the dome the Cloud makes; only fools
With time to waste would trust their molecules
To customs sieves.
                                    I coalesced inside
A booth in Buffalo. A Knotter, Slide
Away, had let us know about a big
Estate sale. We've been after Bloody Sig-
Nature, the Moby Dick of *Deads*, the most
Obscure of Mountain myths, a half-glimpsed ghost
That flits around the edges of the *Knot*.
As diehard Knotters know, it's often thought
James Gordon signed one copy of the single
In his very blood. (He meant to mingle
With his art, or so the story goes.)
The big estate in question—Buffalo's
Great claim to fame, the dude who made the smart-
Wig—interests us because the dude loved art.
Specifically, this wig tycoon collected
Vinyl and, it seems, was quite respected
For his rare and priceless acquisitions.

There was weird shit, smartwig exhibitions,

As you walked inside the outdoor tent:
A poster on what lack of sunlight meant
For hair loss, plus a giant statue of
The dude, a holo that some stupid dove
Kept flapping at. (I think it meant to land;
A wig held by the statue's outstretched hand
Looked like a nest.) Another bird!—but this
One wasn't marked with red.

                       Young men in bliss
Perused the vinyl bins on several tables.
But the Bloody Sig, the stuff of fables,
Would elude me. Frowny face. (Of course,
And unsurprisingly, I couldn't source
A plain old copy either.)

                      As I left,
Sidling through an unofficial cleft
Where two ends of the tent had failed to close,
My tired eyes filled up with postcard prose.
I headed to my booth to vaporize
Myself . . .

           —224 replies.

*   *   *

From *Authors for a Safer World: A Brief
Account*. Part Three. By A. F. Wilson Leaf.

By 2039, they'd cinched a loop
Around their final neck. The terror group
Had turned against their Founder for a post
He'd written in his youth. They watched him roast
And sway—a flaming, thrashing pendulum
Tied to a tree—and linked their hands to hum

A dirge. The group was down to three last members.
(They'd fed their impure elements to embers.)
They hated hate, but saw no irony
In donning masks—or lashing men to trees.
Their real-world names were Kyle, Nate, and Prudence.
All three were Creative Writing students.

The Founder, thrashing, had been their professor.
Murdering a critic was the lesser
Of a pair of evils that included
Snarky book reviewing, he'd concluded.
Snarky book reviews were forms of violence.
Words that harm are worse than airless silence.

The Founder finished fuming. He was dead.
They hiked back to their campsite, where they read
Unpublished poetry and praised each other.

"Musings on a Tintype of My Mother,"
Prudence said. She wore a toque and gripped
A shaky Moleskine. Nate and Kyle flipped
Their eyes to ON. "Record," they said. They each
Wore hoodies, jeans, and beards, and dreamed of teaching
Jobs. Nate's head employed a person bun.
(The sexist coinage "man bun" was a gun-
Shot of a word that made them shake with rage.)

The toque was done. Nate's turn. He held a page
And rattled it and cleared his throat. "The Pyre,"
He said. They sat on logs around a fire,
By their van. "i [sic] / hurl through the air

The torn- / off cocks . . ." They all made sure to stare
At one another, eyes recording, heads
As still as they could make them. Praise-filled threads
Unspooled inside their thoughts. They liked to shoot
Their readings, put them up on ZuckTube's Hoot,
A platform where "Creative Souls" could share
Their stuff. (A bot would like each post and care
About the work. Most users wore a cape.)

The poets hadn't seen the bat-like shape
Above the trees. They'd thought they were alone.
In fact, the bat shape was a Zuck Maps drone
And unbeknownst to them their smarteyes had
Uploaded all that they had seen—their sad
Performances; the sparks the fire shed;
And, swaying from a tree, their Founder, dead—
To Zuck Maps's Forest View, a hiking app.
The next day, hikers calling up a map
Discovered, on a loop, a thrashing man.
Police then traced the tintype to the van
That held the terrorists. They were arrested
Hours later.
        Still, the mind invested
Deeply in what could've been now dwells
On what their many victims—Guriel, Wells,
And others—never got the chance to write:
Non-fiction books of style, wit, and light
About Van Toorn, MT, and more. Parts four
Through fourteen of this brief account explore
My made-up canon of unwritten, must-
Read masterworks like *Jacketed in Dust*,

Brooke Clark's lost study of the peerless *Mountain*
Tea, or Sylvie Simmons's *Last Count In:*
On The Mountain's B-side "Yesterday."
If you have contributions—other grey
Lit for this growing series—please apprise
Me. Thread is open.
                                        —84 replies.

* * *

From "Titles for Imaginary Tracks
By Mountain Tea," by Drew MacLeod.
                                                    The Wax
Museum Melts. Papyrus Blues (Part Four).
Ellipsis. Godless. Dark Room Without Door.
Short Suite with Parts for Gong and Singing Dog.
The Noseless Roman Bust. The War of Fog.
The Sleep Song. Orson Welles's Final Dream.
Unending Cloud. An Ode to Primal Scream.
An Ode to Brian Wilson. Reggae Metal.
Syd Barrett's Frozen Brain. The Flower Petal
Made of Razor. Trunkless Legs of Stone.
An Elegy for Patti D. The Zone.
Cassette Tape Caught like Pubes in Shrubbery
(Part Seven). Scattered Shards of Pottery.
The Robot Rap. Machine Against the Rage.
James Gordon's Ballad. One-Page Book with Page
Torn Out. Afloat at Sea with Thomas Pynchon.
The Bot in Love. The Bot Becomes a Christian.
Clockwork Orange Eyes. Zapruder Tape.
Brief Melody in Key of X. The Rape
Of William Butler Yeats by Several Swans.

A Sound Loop Built from Thirty Thousand Yawns.
The Artist, After Years of Failure, Dies.

—Thread closed. 342 replies.

* * *

From F. R. Furst's "Garage Ontologies:
Absence in the Art for Mountain Tea's
The Dead."
                    The sleeve presents the band's garage,
Where they rehearsed, as Cornell box. Collage.
Our only extant glimpses of this sleeve—
My screen grabs from the clips on ZuckTube—leave
A lot to be desired. But if we pan
Across the grainy composites, we can
Make out LPs dispersed throughout the space,
Plus other objects: boxes, standup bass,
A couple stacks of books, a microphone,
Guitar and cello, vintage Moog, trombone.
A few *Blade Runner*-style zoom-ins bring
Some spines in focus: Alan Moore's *Swamp Thing.*
Pale Fire. The Crying of Lot 49.
Disgrace. The Rocking Chair, by A. M. Klein.
These texts construct a patriarchal canon.
A token girl presides: it's Jackie DeShannon,
Tacked up on a wall and relegated
To the state of muse. The records, weighted
On the side of rock, place godlike rock
Stars at the centre of the world: "Bangkok,"
By Chilton; *Love*, by Love. There's also "Guess
I'm Dumb" (Glen Campbell) next to deep cut "Yes

Sir, That's My Baby" (Hale and the Hushabyes)
And *Godz 2*, with the punk-like "Radar Eyes."
The bands are mostly white. Thus Gordon's taste—
The cover's clearly his work—has erased
The Other. Mountain Tea themselves are out
Of sight, but this erasure serves to flout
Their agency. The band transcends garage
Like absent god. Lost signified. Mirage.
Their name, as well, is nowhere on the sleeve.
It's almost like the band's resolved to leave
Its fate up to the whims of memory.
It's almost like there is no Mountain Tea . . .

5.

The scow came to a stop. The human cabbie—
A novelty these days—said, "That's the abbey."
The face his rearview mirror held was covered
By a cowl. Mute. The scow still hovered
Several feet above the unpaved ground.
The hooded man jumped out. The droning sound
The scow made as it lifted off was soon
Mosquito whine.

              The man looked up. A moon
Was out, but seemed half-hearted—seemed to waver.
Flicker. The abbey's monks had tried to save her
Glow. They aimed recordings at the sky,
False moons that rippled when a scow flew by.
The dark-grey canvas they projected on—
Unending Cloud—conflated dusk and dawn.

One moon, on loop, preserved a bird in flight:
A crow shape crossed the circle twice a night
And blinked out as it passed beyond the orb.
These long-gone moons on tape, forced to absorb
Their long-gone suns and play them back forever,
Gave the abbey's monks, who almost never

Spoke, a voice—projected from the roof.

The hooded figure followed small, twinned hoof-
Prints to the abbey's gate and rang the bell.
The abbey, on a hill, implied a hell:
The valleyed world below. A stone wall, pocked
With moss, went round the abbey. If you walked
Too far along the wall, you'd have to climb;
The wall gave way to cliff. Laid out like time,
The abbey's huts were digits on a clock.
The tower, in the centre, housed the stock
Of dumbprint, plus the large scriptorium,
Where monks, who'd dubbed this "God's Emporium,"
Transcribed the contents of the Zuck by hand.

The gate groaned open. Floating lanterns panned
Their beams across the hooded figure's body.
His dull grey cloak was offset by a gaudy
Detail: bright white, turf-indifferent shoes.

A monk rushed up to meet the figure. "Snooze!"
He cried. The lanterns dimmed and flew away.
The monk—the abbot—spread an arm: this way.
(A monk could speak but only to a bot.)

The abbot showed the guest his hut. One cot.
Small table. Towel. Charger cord. The cowl
Allowed the slightest nod.
                              Outside, a howl
Flared up, plateaued, and died: self-flagellating
Monk, or wolf, or worse—the mind conflating
Several different selves, or beasts, in pain.

The abbot took his leave. A hoarse refrain
Of howl bassooned—then stopped. As if cut off.
Silence. A neighbouring hut produced a cough.

The guest sat on the cot, removed his cowl.
Egg-shaped glass: a bot. It took the towel
And wiped a film of dust and fingerprints.
A pixelated face in bluish tints.
The face the towel polished wore a pair
Of glasses normally.
                    A wall of hair
Displaced the face, now turned to peer behind
The bot, as if a face could have a mind
All of its own. It turned and swept the space
For traces of a man who'd once played bass.

* * *

They'd had, the café's smartbooks, more to say.
When Gibson was alone inside Swann's Way,
The walls would whirlpool into words and clauses,
Then go white, creating natural pauses
Where he could reply. He'd pan his thoughts
Across the Wheel of Fortune walls; the bots
Inside the books he eyed would drag his mind
And catch his drift. Each book, bright white, re-spined
Itself, transforming into *Mountain Tea*,
The Véhicule edition from '03,
With sky-blue spine. What *else* could Gibson paint
His words with?
                Still, he felt the strict constraint
Of building letters from such slender blocks.
His unseen correspondent—H. U. Hawks!—

Was likely at a keyboard, typing out
His thoughts, which ate up walls and seemed to flout
His speed. For his part, Gibson found that "I"s
Were easy. But he had to pan his eyes
In clockwise circles when it came to "O"s.
And "M"s took time. This way of writing prose
Was wicked work—like setting type by hand
Or reproducing *Finnegans Wake* in sand.
He found he often had to use a wall
Per letter, meaning one whole word would sprawl
Throughout *Swann's Way*, the wooden shelves implying
Lines on foolscap, the giant word complying
With the stave that ran straight through. (The bot-
Barista, busy wiping mugs, was not
Attuned, it seemed, to what this roiling frieze
Was up to.)
               Hawks was shocked that Mountain Tea's
One single had inspired such devotion;
He'd been offzuck for years. "TOO MUCH COMMOTION,"
The walls explained. "I NEEDED SILENCE. TIME
TO THINK."
               But then the door ahem-ed; the chime
That signalled someone's entrance was a cough—
A hack by Jonathan Franzen—lifted off
The audio of a birding lecture given
Years ago. The dialogue was riven.
The walls went white—then quickly pixellated,
As books with different spines repopulated
The shelves. A tourist wandered in and smiled.

They spoke this way for weeks, their chats defiled
By Franzen's frequent cough. When customers

Came in, the chat would end. "The guy prefers
An empty room," said Gibson, when he told
Hayes what was happening.

                      "You've got to hold
Him," Hayes said. "Keep him hooked."

                              Hawks talked of life
Post-Mountain Tea. The booze. The drugs. The wife
Who left him. Tears. Rock bottom. Then the missile.
The one that sounded like a distant whistle
Or spooky theremin. The one Don Jr
Ordered, reducing Montréal to lunar
Crater. The grass that wouldn't grow again.
The lives erased. The growths that grew on men.
The one- to three-eyed kids. As if to mark
A mournful mood, the smartbook spines went dark.

He talked of starting over. ("MEDITATION!")
He saw an angel in a dream. ("SALVATION!")

"I LOVED ART. LEARNED COMPUTERS. HOW TO CODE.
TO HACK. I GOT A KIND OF DESK JOB. SLOWED
RIGHT DOWN." Years passed. Hawks found the retrospective
In MOJO ("LUCK!") and then the fan collective
("SOMETHING KNOT"), which led him to Swann's Way's
Café; the site said Gibson spent his days
There.

        "HOW THO," wondered Gibson, "R U SPEAKING?"
(He'd stopped at "H"; it took a lot of tweaking,
Italicizing words.)

                    A single, narrow
Line extended, book by book, an arrow
At its tip. It crossed the room and wound

Up pointing at the bot-barista's round
And one-eyed head. "I HACKED THE CAFE BOT.
ACCESSED ITS EYE. YOU CAN AIM A THOUGHT
BY WAY OF BOT STRAIGHT AT THE SMARTBOOK WALL."
The bot, oblivious, an upright doll—
Or so it seemed—was swabbing at a table,
Attached to Hawks by way of unseen cable.
Hawks was mum on why he felt compelled
To *think* shapes into words. But Gibson held
His tongue; he would've used two string-bound cans
To talk to Hawks.

       "YOUR FRIENDS ARE FERVENT FANS,"
Said Hawks one day. "BUT THEY SHOULD LOOK TO GOD
FOR MEANING." Gibson thought that sounded odd.
Increasingly, Hawks steered their conversation
To Satan. Hell. The dangers of temptation.
At one point, one long row of books turned rose
In colour. Then, it split to span three rows,
The rose line forking like a pitchfork's tines.
Above these tines, implying pulsing lines
Of heat, a few spines throbbed. "WE MUST DESIRE
GOD, NOT FAME, OR ELSE WERE BOUND FOR FIRE."

Gibson tried to steer him back. "BUT WHAT
ABOUT THE DEAD? DO U HAV COPIES?"

          "IVE SHUT
THAT DOOR," said Hawks. Whenever Gibson brought
Up Gordon's band, the walls went blank or got
Evasive. "LETS NOT TALK OF MOUNTAIN TEA."

But then one day: "WE CUT A GREAT LP
YOU KNOW. BUT GORDON COULDNT BRING HIMSELF

TO PUT IT OUT. HE LEFT IT ON THE SHELF.
THATS WHEN THE BAND SPLIT UP."
                                    They'd been recording
A full-length album, after years of hoarding
And refining songs. But Gordon balked
At every take. In time, the singer walked.
Then Lou, their crack guitarist. That left Hawks
Who'd played both bass and drums. The album rocks,
He tried to say to Gordon. Let's just mix
The thing and get it out. By that point, six
Whole years had passed, *The Dead* their one release.

"THE ALBUM WOULDVE BEEN A MASTERPIECE.
BUT GORDON BURNED IT. CASE OF SOUR GRAPES."

And then, one afternoon: "I STILL HAVE TAPES
YOU KNOW. THE HEATHEN THOUGHT HED BURNED THEM ALL.
BUT I MADE COPIES." Something crossed the wall:
A smile?
            That's all the spines would ever say;
The Franzen cough ahem-ed their chat away
And Hawks, it seemed, decided he was done.
Days passed. Then weeks. The shelves of books stayed mum.

* * *

By 5 a.m., the monks had shuffled off
To mass, a horse attending to a trough
The only life around. They hadn't turned
Their blazing sun on yet: bespoke, it burned
Above the hill all day.
                        The bot explored
The quiet, foggy grounds. It walked toward

The abbey's central tower, placed its shoe
Upon the brickwork, waited for a few
More seconds—'til the turf-indifferent sole
Produced an all-good beep—then took a stroll
Straight up the bricks, its dull grey cloak a curtain
Panel hanging limp. The bot, uncertain
When the mass would end, picked up its pace.
Its cowl had slipped off its glassy face,
Revealing Gibson's visage in the egg.
The bot trod heavily; it stomped each leg
Emphatically to try to stick the tread.
The bot was light as styrofoam, its head
The heavy part, so when it stopped before
What looked to be a chasm in the floor—
A window facing west—it seemed to shiver
As a tree branch, long and taut, will quiver.

It kneeled and gripped the window's upper edge,
Then swung its legs across the stony ledge
And dropped into a room, behind a barrel:
Abbey ale. It crouched like something feral.
Looked around. Its glowing head had lit
The gloomy space—which duly dimmed a bit
When Gibson made the bot pull up its hood.
Throughout the room stood casks of weathered wood.

"Hayes," said Gibson. "Take the wheel." The bot's
Face scrambled; Hayes's face resolved, his thoughts
Now threaded through the musculature of
The bot, his hand inside a mock-flesh glove.

* * *

Hayes and Gibson, sitting at a table
Far away, were still. Two ink-black cables
Streamed from each man's pupils; four in all
Ran to a rented iStage disc. A doll-
Scale bot (a holo of the real one) jogged
In place upon the disc. Both men were logged
In through their eyes. It almost looked as if
Their pupils had distended, then turned stiff.
Their brains' instructions to the bot coursed through
The cables; think to raise an arm and two
Went up—the holo version, on the disc,
And, critically, the one that took the risk
Of being real, out in the world, the one
Now moving through the tower with a gun
Wand, Hayes's, in its grip. Hayes assured
Them he had set its slender shaft to herd
Mode, which meant crowd control.

                                    Hayes had hacked
The bot-barista's eye. In time, he'd tracked
Their man to Hilltop Rose, a monastery
In Scotland. Hilltop Rose's monks were wary
Of the flesh; all tourists had to use
A bot. Those wanting access to the views
Provided by the abbey—Zuckgram stars—
Were often turned away. They'd hire cars,
Drive up the hill, and storm the property
In search of perfect selfies. Scholarly
Intentions, though, could get you in, so Hayes
And Gibson spent a couple anxious days
DMing with the site's administrators.
They'd sold themselves as serious curators

Of illuminated, handmade zlogs.
The men were told they'd have to sign some logs,
Employ a bot, and absolutely *not*
Talk to the monks.

                              With funding from the *Knot*,
They flew to Glasgow, holing up with Drew
MacLeod. His "covers" band, The Avian Flu,
Made counterfeits: imaginary songs
For Mountain Tea, strange songs with sitars, gongs,
An Ondes Martenot (an early keyboard filled
With vacuum tubes), and such. The unfulfilled
Potential of James Gordon's band inspired
Drew, who *was* The Avian Flu; he'd fired
All his bandmates in the Gordonesque
Pursuit of perfect tracks. His mixing desk
(Where Drew was fussing with assorted takes
His band had left behind, well-meaning fakes
That dreamed The Mountain into being) faced
The table where both Hayes and Gibson (spaced
Out, plugged in) had been piloting the rental.

Gibson, taking care to be as gentle
As he could, teased out the iStage cable
From each pupil. Placed them on the table.
His armless glasses, floating near his head
Like flotsam, flew straight over to his red
And heavy eyelids.

                              "Welcome back," said Drew,
Head down. He lifted steaming coffee. Blew.

His loft had hardwood floors; some rain-filled pots;
A ripped settee whose stuffing foamed in spots

(Where Drew slept); sleeping bags, two recent buys
(Where Hayes and Gibson slept); and camp supplies.

"You look like shit," said Drew, his head still down.
He wore a torn High Llamas t-shirt, frown,
And stubble.
                    Hayes stayed focused, stationary,
The bot still moving through the monastery
Tower. Hayes had turned a filter on;
The doll-sized holo of the bot—a wan
Projection—had become a Gundam, studded
With a riot of assorted rudders.
Two articulated hands were trying
Unseen doors. It looked like it was flying;
Its feet began an inch above the iStage.

"Well," said Gibson. "When you get to my age,
Bot-walks take a toll."
                    Drew looked at him.
He knew why Gibson always looked so grim,
But no one ever mentioned Gibson's wife
And son. It was a rule: he had no life
Before The Mountain.
                    Gibson looked around.
"There coffee?"
                    "By the sink." A sawing sound
Was groaning in the loft—old cello parts
That Drew was mulling over.
                    Several charts
For strings, with scribbled notes, were strewn across
Drew's kitchen counter. Gibson noted sauce-
Webbed forks. A pile of takeout styrofoam

Iceflowing from the trash. He found a chrome
Carafe—the only thing that Drew would deign
To rinse—and poured himself a mug. A brain-
Sized heap of old chow mein was thinking in
The microwave. Drew's bandmates hadn't been
Around for months.

                "Hey, check this out," said Hayes.
"I'll switch the POV." A chunky blaze
Of pixels flared. The Gundam was replaced
By Hayes's view: a room whose stained glass faced
And filtered phony sunlight. Wooden desks
Were ranked, the holo scene shot through with specks
Of dust from Drew's loft. Every desk included
Vellum and a laptop. Quills protruded
From quill holes, as if the desks had plumage.
Other tools lay scattered: inkhorns, pumice
Stones (to smooth the vellum), knives, and rulers.
Apparently the monks, like careful jewellers,
Copied zlogs their abbot judged of worth
Straight off the Zuck: stray works of grace and mirth,
Which pop-up pamphlets, pest-like, often wiped
Away.

      The bot bent over vellum striped
With stained-glass sunlight. (Gibson had to look
Away a sec; the view plunged fast.) The book
Its scribe was slowly crafting seemed to be
Composed of ancient Yelp reviews. "This Sea
Salt Ice Cream Is The Bomb," the parchment read,
Green ivy winding through the words like thread
And joining up with foliage that framed
The page. Another manuscript proclaimed,
"*Last Jedi*? Yup, It's Canon"—"*L*" and "*J*"

So large the small print circled them the way
A stream will snake past stones.

                              Beside each text,
The laptop showed the source: a cellphone sext,
For instance, like a sonnet by John Donne,
Or someone's op-ed, from the *Times*, for gun
Control.

               The vertigo-inducing gaze,
Which veered and swung erratically as Hayes
Went desk to desk, had now paused on a screen
Set to a page from MOJO magazine.
The monk in question had been writing out
A copy of a piece—the one about
The Mountain from the 2037
Issue, attributed to "Patti Devin."

"Jesus Christ," said Hayes. "Our friend's been busy."
Hayes's darting eyes made Gibson dizzy.
The scribe had drawn the figures in the tintype.
Cherubs hung about his page's thin white
Border, each one armed with horn and flag.
He'd made a work of art out of the mag.

A bell began to toll. The bot's view veered
Away. With every step, the world appeared
To heave and lurch. The bot took up behind
A heavy arras. Soon the monks assigned
To copy filed in.

                    By this point, Drew
Had sidled up to Gibson. "Shitty view,"
He said. The holo, solid black, displayed
The arras.

"Just a sec," said Hayes. He made
The bot peer out a bit. "That better now?"

"A lot," said Drew.
                    Each monk had made a vow
Of silence; scraped-out chairs composed the only
Noise. When all were seated, one last lonely
Monk came in and sat before the waiting
MOJO, which he'd been illuminating.
"A KIND OF DESK JOB"—that had been the phrase.
Behind the monk, the stained glass was ablaze.

"Zoom in a bit," said Gibson. Hayes refreshed
The view. The monk went blocky—pixel-fleshed—
But Gibson knew the swarm of skin-tone blocks
Was Mountain Tea's bass player, Hal U. Hawks.

* * *

Hayes snuck back to the hut and tried to keep
His cool. He parked the bot, which went to sleep.

Back in the loft, the men devised a plan.
They'd wait 'til Hawks was sleeping. Then, they'd scan
His hut for tapes—a copy of *The Dead*,
Of course, and next, the album Hawks had said
Was nearly finished. Gibson wanted so
Much more—to really talk to Hawks, to know
His mind. But clearly Hawks had said his piece.
His unheard music was his masterpiece.

Hayes lay down for a nap. Drew worked on tracks.
And Gibson wandered Glasgow, with The Yaks,

A Mountain "covers" band, inside his ears.
(He favoured old-school earbuds shaped like tears.)
He often walked for hours on his own
Through Tokyo. He liked to be alone
On foot, a city's flow of info streaming
By, the earbuds drowning out the screaming
Of his wife and son. But Glasgow's solid
Sandstone buildings loomed. They seemed too stolid.
Stubborn even. History had dug
Its heels in here; the stonework seemed to lug
A sense of long-gone life, its chiselled detail
Dense. He passed a church, a stretch of retail
Shops, and cloudy Zubers. Overhead,
The sun was out of focus. It had bled
A bit along its edge, like egg yolk smeared.
(The city's artificial light appeared
To be a little glitchy.) As he walked,
He startled flocks of pigeons, which re-flocked,
And watched his image ripple on the liquid
Glass of storefronts.
                              Back at Drew's, insipid
Beats were throbbing. Hayes was in the shower.
Drew stood by a window. "This one's 'Flower
On a Hill'," he said. He didn't turn
His head. Perhaps he was performing yearning,
Gazing at the street. "I'm trying drum
Machines and synths." His hand began to strum
His stomach as the sound of someone's bass—
Drew's ex, Flu bassist Alice X, her face
A tattoo on his neck—kicked in and started
Pulsing.
                    Gibson said, "It's . . . new. Uncharted

Ground for you."
                    A minute passed, Drew staring
Out the window. "This part's rather daring."
An orchestra broke in for one brief bar:
A crashing chord. Drew ceased his air guitar.
He frowned. "I'm not sure we should hear *The Dead*."

Gibson looked at him, the Scotsman's head
Still staring at the street. "What makes you think
That now?"
              Drew met his eyes. The dark-blue ink
Composing Alice X's face began
To transform slowly. "Gordon's just a man,
You know." The ink had stalled, the tattoo Miró-
Like. "Perhaps you shouldn't hear your hero."

* * *

They took a more official site tour later.
The face of Hilltop's site administrator,
A monk who'd yet to take his vows, appeared
Inside their loft. Its hair was bowl-shaped, sheared
An inch or so above the ear. It floated
Just above the iStage, looking bloated:
A peephole face, the resolution blurry.
"Hello?" it said. It squinted.
                                  "Gibs, please hurry,"
Said Hayes, as Gibson plugged each eye and logged
Back in.
           The monk, his face in close, had fogged
The bot's head up a little (which is why
The face was blurred). He stepped back as one eye
Appeared upon the glass—and then the rest

Of Gibson's face. The rental, not the best
Bot you could get, was laggy.
                                        As they toured
The grounds, the monk held forth. "Our monks are lured
Here by the promise of a holy life,"
He said. "They've taken parchment for a wife
And look for God in godless works of praise."
A sun, above, suggested sun-like rays.

The monks were artisans, but hackers, too,
Their tour guide said. They scraped away the glue
That plastered over zucksites: pop-up pamphlets
On the Deep State, say, encasing Hamlet's
Speeches on some drama student's zlog.

"We like to say we clear away the fog
That's drifted over human memory,"
The monk explained. "We salvage poetry,
Impassioned book reviews. Last week, an ode
To poutine. We can crack through any code."

Inside the writing room, the monks were still
At work. The MOJO monk, hood up, seemed ill.
He sat there, shoulders hunched, his body shaking.
Earlier, the iStage zoom kept making
Hawks—assuming it was Hawks—resemble
Pixels. Gibson hadn't caught the tremble
In his hands. The monk pulled out a drawer—
His spastic rifling rattling the floor—
And found a shaky ruler. Gibson brought
His own hood up, to hide the face his bot
Displayed. He cleared his throat.

                                             "That man," he said
And nodded, "looks unwell." Like he'd been bled
Of blush.
                    The tour guide tsk'ed. "He broke his vow
Of silence."
                         Gibson, feigning calm, said, "How?"

The MOJO monk had been assigned some prose
To copy for the shelves of Hilltop Rose.
By chance, the text—an essay—praised a band
The monk had been in once. "I think God planned
To test him," said the guide. "Such things awaken
Old ambitions. Brother Hawks was shaken
To discover he had devotees."
(Back in the loft, Drew traded looks with Hayes,
As both men watched the holo.) "Hawks snuck in
This room one night," the guide explained. "A sin."
He sat down at a terminal and went
Onzuck. He later claimed he'd never meant
To break his vow; he'd found a way to speak
His mind without a voice. "The flesh is weak,"
The guide said, sighing. "Brother Hawks was given
A 'talk.'" (Air quotes.) "He's feeling *slightly* shriven."

* * *

That evening, Gibson piloting, they crept
Up on the hut where Hawks, exhausted, slept.
They heard a crack of leather—then a howl.
Gibson moved in closer, pulled the cowl
Off, and peered in.
                         Hawks knelt on the floor.
His back, which faced the door, displayed a score

Of lash marks. It looked like a cutting board.
His right arm, rigid, held a hilt. A cord
Whip-cracked across his back, then drew away
Around his neck, as Hawks prepared to flay
Himself again, his arm extending out.
Gibson, hand raised, couldn't help but shout
A "No!" The shirtless body startled. Swivelled.

And there, now facing Gibson, deeply chiselled—
Wrinkled—was the man just second from
The left in MOJO's tintype, poised to strum
Some long-lost double bass. But *this* man, streaming
Tears, was not the man whom Gibson, dreaming
Of this day for ages, had expected.
(It was as if the double bass, dejected,
Had gone flaccid, softened into whip.)

"It's me," said Gibson. "Gibson." Hawks's lip
Was quivering. He shook his head.

                                        "I can't."
He waved the whip. "They'll force me to recant."
He struck his chest and cried, "Please go!" Then struck
His chest again. Again.

                            "Jesus fuck,"
Cried Drew, recoiling from the iStage holo.

Hawks pushed past, and Gibson turned to follow.
Felt confused. His limbs were moving, but
His view, fixed on the wall inside the hut,
Was frozen.

                    "Fucking Wi-Fi dropped," said Hayes.
He shook the iStage. Gibson tried to raise

An arm. The bot, its head lolled to the side,
Was limp.
            "Reboot!" said Drew.
                              "I've fucking tried,"
Said Hayes.
            A minute passed. The bot exploded
Into action; Gibson had spring-loaded
It, by flailing frantically, with pent-up
Gestures. (It moved the way a man on sped-up
Tape might.) When it settled, Gibson steered
It through the doorway. Everything appeared
Bright green. Night vision.
                        Over by the cliff,
A man-shaped form seemed trapped inside a gif,
Attempting squats, as if about to leap.
Years after, Gibson saw it in his sleep:
The half-crouched silhouette of Hal U. Hawks
Rehearsing how he'd leap upon the rocks.

* * *

They stayed until the morning so as not
To raise suspicion. Gibson parked the bot
Back in their hut. Hayes felt it best to leave
The bassist's hut untouched; some might perceive
A theft as murder-motive. Gibson felt
That going in Hal's hut would leave a welt
Across their souls. And Drew was mostly quiet.

At one point, Hayes said, "Think the monks will buy it?"

Gibson, on Drew's floor, stared at the ceiling.
He spoke at last. "They know that Hawks was feeling

Desperate. There's no good reason to connect
Our visit to his jump. They don't suspect
Us."

      Each one tried to dodge the other's gaze.
They waited out the night and watched the day's
First rays of artificial sunlight creep
Across Drew's floor.

                A voice. "Are you asleep?"

Gibson plugged back in and found the site
Administrator in their hut.

                "Last night,"
He said, "a monk passed."

             Gibson mustered shock.
"Oh no . . ." The monk said he had had to walk
From hut to hut, explaining what had taken
Place.

      "A suicide," he said, with graven
Shaking of his sheared and bowl-shaped hair.
He crossed himself and said the briefest prayer.
"Remember Brother Hawks, the one you pointed
Out?" He tsk'ed; he sounded disappointed.
"We found his body lying on a shelf
Of rock. He'd fallen there." Re-crossed himself.

"But maybe," Gibson offered, "Brother Hawks
Fell off the cliff by accident?" A box
Beneath the site administrator's arm
Caught Gibson's eyes.

           "We think he meant to harm
Himself." The site administrator sighed.
"A written note we found confessed he'd tried

And failed to spurn material desire.
It said we should commit his things to fire."

"What things?" asked Gibson.
                              "Personal possessions,"
The site administrator said. "Obsessions
That obscured God's love. Some ancient reels
Of tape." The sky above rang out with peals,
The tower tolling.
                  Nodding at the box,
Gibson said, "Is that what Brother Hawks
Was haunted by?" He felt a distant palm—
Hayes's—grip his shoulder.
                          In a calm,
Bright voice, the site administrator said,
"Oh no, we've burned those. One was labelled, 'Dead,'
I think. And one said, 'Album,' I believe."
The site administrator took his leave.

6.

From *Void: A Film about The Avian Flu.*

"They played live once, before MacLeod withdrew
From touring." Cut to seated figure dressed
In desert scarves. A caption—Hashtag Blessed,
Fine Artist—fades in just below. The man
Holds up scene-setting hands. "The Flu began
With backs turned to the crowd." Dissolve to grainy
Footage: a band on stage. "The show was brainy.
Moving." Four musicians face a blown-
Up tintype from the MOJO piece—the lone
Existing shot of Mountain Tea. "They played
That way, heads down, all night. The way men prayed
To gods once." Shaky handheld footage. Poor sound.
Heads hunched over gear. A crop of foreground
Arms consumes their lower halves, a thicket
Of front-row limbs.

           New voice: "I lost my ticket..."
The film cuts to a different talking head,
A blazered, bear-like man, whose pelt is red,
Two paws upon his lap. "...But I was there."
His pinstriped dress shirt's collar blooms with hair.

His head seems buoyed on a shaggy platter.
"There aren't a lot of shows that really matter.
This one did." The film runs through some shots
Of Drew MacLeod on stage, a swarm of dots
Supplying newsprint-grey tone. Back to furry
Man. "The label, though, began to worry.
Its big investment was procrastinating."
His claw-tipped paws are now gesticulating,
A caption fading in: J. Marcus Gates,
Rolling Stone. "They'd miss recording dates.
They'd throw out every take. I think, in part,
The Flu were doing, like, performance art."
He claws his mane. "These guys were gonna be"—
Quick cut to MOJO tintype—"Mountain Tea."
The shot zooms slowly in. "Perfectionists."

A bearded man. "The Flu? Postmodernists.
Tricksters." Dr Fulton West, Professor
Of Pop Culture, Yale. "They weren't some lesser
Tribute band. They were a meta band.
And pissing off the label? That was planned.
They meant to sabotage their work, their sessions."
Cut to shots of artists whose obsessions
Helped condemn them—Spector, Kubrick, Welles,
And Lauryn Hill—to private, inner hells.
"They meant to be a self-defeating group.
They meant to waste three months on one brief loop
Of drums. Demand rare mixing desks. Ignore all
Good advice." A still of Andy Warhol
Fills the screen. "It was a kind of pop
Art thing. Conceptual."

* * *

                         "Drew wouldn't stop
Recording." Cut. A woman in a pair
Of off-white frames, a Raincoats tee. Her hair,
A pulsing bob, is slowly cycling through
The rainbow. Alice X, The Avian Flu,
Guitar, Viola, Bass—the list so long
Her caption takes a smaller font. "One song
We worked on"—Alice sighs—"it felt like ages.
Drew descended into violent rages
When we didn't sound the way it did
Up here." She taps her bob. Her hair has slid
Into a darker palette, browns and greys,
As if to match her tone. "One day he'd praise
You, say you sounded brilliant..." Cut to B-
Roll: mixing desk, and on it, cups of tea,
Sound levels up and downing like unstable
Skylines. Drew, cross-legged on a table,
Furiously writing. Random dials. Wires.
Cut back to Alice X, her smartwig's fibres
Solid black. A void. "...And then he'd tear
You down. It wasn't just for show, though." Hair
Now growing orange like an oven, passion
In her voice. "It wasn't." Pause. "It's fashion-
Able to think that, maybe." Alice looks
Off to the side.

                         Cut back to Gates. "Drew hooks
In people who will subsidize The Flu
And keep him going. Benefactors who
Will fund his life." He laces furry paws
Together. "Often ends quite badly." Pause.

"But Drew can charm you."

                        Alice. "Well, the first
Time we hung out, just after we'd rehearsed,
Drew made me watch the Orson Welles *Othello*.
Projected on his wall." She laughs. "Um, hello,
1951." Her eyes look down.
She smiles to herself. But then, a frown.
"He said he wished he could've lived back then.
In Welles's time"—a mock-gruff voice—"When Men
Made Works of Art." She looks up. "We were on
His old settee. We talked all night. 'Til dawn.
Most men I know, they would've filled that loft
With holo statues. Scarface. Lara Croft.
But Drew just had the mixing desk, settee,
Projector, and a poster: *La Jetée*."

An off-screen voice asks something.

                           "Why *Othello*?"
She repeats. (A theme begins. A cello.)
She thinks about it. "Well, you know, it meant
A lot to him. Drew said that Welles had spent
His acting money making it. He'd leave
The set to take a job. 'Can you believe
That?' Drew would say. 'To have to leave your cast
And crew for weeks?' But once Welles had amassed
Enough, the shoot resumed. The film took years
To make, which blew Drew's mind. 'Such sweat and tears,'
He'd say in awe." Dissolve to shots of Welles
As Alice talks. "Welles stitched together cells
Of film he'd shot in different places *and*
At different times. He used, like, sleight of hand
To slip shit by you. One scene, Welles deployed

These lances—which were toothpicks. From a void,
He plucked a world. And that inspired Drew.
And Drew, the way he talked, inspired you.
Or me, I guess." Cut back to Alice X.
"But anyway." Her bob is streaked with flecks
Of gold. "The sun turned on. He touched my wrist."

The off-screen voice asks something.
                              "Yeah, we kissed,"
She says.
              Cut back to Dr Fulton West.
"He *loved* Welles." Several shots from films, distressed,
Flash by—a bearded Welles made up like Shylock;
Scenes from *Don Quixote*—each on film stock
Of a different provenance. "Welles started
Many films, but backers often parted
Ways with him. Drew loved to dream about
These partial works. The sort of texts that flout
Their greatness, but—and here's the sneaky part—
Will never have to prove it. That's the art
Drew longed to make. Unfinished masterpieces."
Cut to ruins, Roman busts in pieces,
Swiss-cheesed parchment.

* * *

                              Cut to Hashtag Blessed.
"He met me at my Zuber. Drew was dressed
In old Adidas, jeans, a *Neuromancer*
Tee with holes. 'That shit'll give you cancer,'
He said—he meant the booth I'd just stepped out of.
That week in Glasgow, Drew would often spout off
On the dangers of technology.

His album, *Unmade Songs of Mountain Tea*,
Was nearly done, and I was there to work
On cover art."
                    The off-screen voice.
                                        "Berserk?"
Says Hashtag Blessed. "I guess I wouldn't frame
It *that* way. Look, the whole band was to blame
For what went down." Interiors of Drew's
Loft. "We were listening to 'Papyrus Blues'
Around Drew's mixing desk." Assorted stills
Of men hunched over. Bottles. Glasses. Pills.
"The Flu were there. Just hanging out. Like, proud
That someone—me—could hear their work. A cloud
Hung over Drew, I'll grant. He seemed impatient.
He wanted *Unmade*'s sleeve to look like ancient
Paper—that's *why* he'd played the song 'Papyrus
Blues'."
            The shot begins to slowly iris
Out. The screen goes black. Guitars begin
To chime; a voice, to wail. It's like it's in
A vast and cave-like space, the voice, a whale-
Shaped studio at sea. (Of course, the wail
Is Drew MacLeod's.) Some kettle drums supply
The rumbling of thunder. Strings imply
A veil of rain, vibrato adding shimmer.
A plectrumed '60s bass begins to simmer
Like a riff by long-dead Carole Kaye.
It seems to writhe beneath the track the way
A snake will ripple sand.
                                    Hashtag Blessed
Breaks in. "It was a masterpiece. Their best
Track. Almost gospel." Church bells start to peal.

Dissolve. Generic shot of reel-to-reel
In motion. "Drew, though, well, he sort of flips."
One reel has reached its end; a tape end whips
The empty air, continuing to spin.
"He slams the mixing desk. 'The bass is thin,'
He says. He starts in playing with the knobs."

The film cuts back to Alice X, her bob's
Smartfibres churning like a time-lapse cloud.
"He'd turned 'Papyrus Blues' up really loud.
His head was in his hands. Kept saying, 'No.'
Like, over and over. 'No.' I tried to show
Support. 'It's great,' I told him."

                                Hashtag Blessed.
"He *sort* of threw a mic stand."

                                Fulton West.
"But if a man were trying to be like
James Gordon, well, he'd *want* to hurl a mic
Stand at his bandmates, wouldn't he? He'd *want*
To end things."

                    Hashtag Blessed. "A true savant—
That's Drew, full stop. He simply couldn't stand
A flaw. So, no, the outburst wasn't planned."

West. "The mic stand comes to represent
The phallus. Violence. Questions of consent.
Artistic passion." Cut to shots of Woody
Allen. Kanye West in dark-grey hoodie.
Byron. Morrissey. "The male auteur
Transcends our social norms, his gestures 'pure.'
'Authentic.'"

      *   *   *

            Gates. "There was a theory Drew
Had fallen in with zealous fans who knew
Where Hawks was—Hal Hawks, bassist for The Mountain."
Cut to Orson Welles, who cries, "the fountain
Of your blood / Is stopp'd," from his *Macbeth*,
Then back to Gates. "Some say they'd caused Hal's death
And Drew had been involved." The film dissolves
To MOJO's article. The shot revolves
And, as Gates narrates, zooms in on the tintype
Of the band—then even further in
On Hawks, still standing second from the left,
With bass in hand. To Hawks's left, bereft
Of grin: the singer, Byrne. To *his* left and
Now nearly out of frame, a guy whose hand
Is forked in V-sign: Reid. To Hawks's right,
Now gone because the shot has gone in tight,
James Gordon. "Certain hardcore fans have said
Drew found Hal in an abbey. Left him dead.
A wild theory." Back to Gates. "I've tried
To dig around. Drew *was* preoccupied
For several months. He'd burned some bridges, fired
His bandmates."
                Alice X. "He'd gone and hired
This artist, Hashtag Blessed. At first, it was
To do the cover, build up album buzz.
But then Drew had this guy, like, follow him
Around and document his life." A hymn-
Like chorus, angels cooing, now starts up.
We cut to several shots of Drew with cup
Aloft before a feast, surrounded by
His acolytes.

"I'd film it with my eye,"
Says Hashtag Blessed. Head back, he pulls his cheeks
And droppers both his pupils. Blinks. Two streaks
Of fluid cross his face. He swabs the tears
Away. "I'd snag the sound"—he tugs his ears—
"With these. My duty was to history."

New footage. Night. Drew reading poetry:
"Shake off the crazies! Sober up, Li Po!"
The book he holds gives off its own warm glow
To read by. Drew is standing on a podium
Outside, young men arrayed around, the sodium
Lights—a parking lot's?—afizz with frantic
Moths.
      Alice. "It all seemed so romantic.
But then his mood would pivot. Even though
The band was gone, I tried to let him know
That *I* was there. That I . . ." She breaks off. Shots
Of Drew now follow: bearded, flanked by bots,
And leading something like a caravan
Deep into jungle. Just behind, a man—
It's Hashtag Blessed—is gesturing to Sherpa
Types. We cut to Drew's attempt to burp a
Baby, which a villager has handed
Him. "He'd gotten Christ-like and demanded
Love. He'd called his fans to help him source
The perfect place"—dissolve to Drew on horse-
Back, waving on a horde of followers—
"To cut 'The Dead.' His version."
                Men in furs
Are sitting next to Drew, inside a hut.
A local makes a motion like a cut;

He's demonstrating something with a blade.
The hut is conical in shape and made,
At first glance, of a 2-D sheet of brush
And fronds. (The sheet is liquid glass and flush
Against the jungle, which is splayed out flat
Against the hut.) Drew wears a light-beige hat,
Safari-style. Next to him, the local
Cups his hands and demonstrates a vocal
Thing. "Is that the way you signal to
A distant tribe?" Drew's caption says in lieu
Of audio. The local shakes his head
And points: it looks as if an arrowhead
Is pressing on the jungle's other side.
A snout appears. A bot has nosed aside
A fold of 2-D world and pushed its way
Inside the hut. It pants and wants to play.
The local strokes its chrome hide with the knife.

Cut back to Alice X. "He said his life
Had no room for a woman. This was in
His loft. We hadn't talked for weeks. He'd been
Out on his grand location scout—a quest
Across the Amazon. His consort, Blessed,
Was in the kitchen, cooking. 'Maybe one
Day this can work,' said Drew. He'd put on *Fun
House*. Kept"—sighs—"interrupting me to draw
Attention to some riff. His constant awe—
It got annoying. Every fucking dude
I've known just wants to brosplain art. Or brood.
I said, 'I love you.'" (Her bob is now a heart's
Dark red.) "'I have to rerecord your parts,'

Was his response. That's when I left. And that
Was that." Dissolve to video of hat
Trunks piled in a boat, Drew steering, plumed
With leafy headdress. "Drew, of course, resumed
His quest," says Alice X. "And I got back
To writing."

Drew is trudging on a track.
He lifts an arm, machetes fronds. We see
His head push through a wall of green. (A pre-
Placed camera—journo drone—is there to snag
The shot.) We watch him sit down, tear a rag,
And bind a wound. Cut to a clearing, Drew
Declaiming from a book, the film shot through
With flickers: micro-blackouts caused whenever
Hashtag's smarteyes blink. "The Grand Endeavor,"
Voice-overed Alice X. "That's what he called
His quest." Drew shuts the book. "And so he walled
Himself away." The song 'Papyrus Blues'
Swells up—then dwindles.

* * *

Gates. "And then the news
Came out. Big news. All caps. A private eye,
Retained by Mountain fans, had found out why
Band members Louis Reid and Dennis Byrne
Had never surfaced." Breath. "He'd come to learn
That Reid and Byrne had died together in
A teleporter accident. Their skin"—
He laces paws—"had fused together." Cut to shot
Of homepage with the banner *Gordian Knot*,
Then to a post whose title reads, "A Piece

Of Puzzle Falls in Place: Please Rest in Peace,
L. Reid, D. Byrne." "Turns out," says Gates, "that 'Reid'
And 'Byrne' were pseudonyms. It seems 'Lou Reed'—
Two 'e's, the guy from Velvet Underground—
Inspired 'Louis Reid.' My guess? They found
The other name by splicing 'David Byrne'
With 'Dennis Wilson.'" B-roll shots. The churn
Of waves. A stretch of desert. Time-lapse, racing
Clouds. "So fans had spent a decade tracing
Men they couldn't find because the names
Were fake." The B-roll has moved on to flames
Consuming parchment. "Hugh McPhee and Clyde
M. Katz. Those were their real names. But they died
In 2036, before there was
A fan base."

          Hashtag Blessed picks at some fuzz
That mars his desert scarves, then looks down at
A book—a very thin one. Coughs.

                        "'fate spat
Their atoms out, / poor reid and byrne, / who passed
Too soon. / the zuber booth, their hell!, amassed
Their molecules, / and lo! / it blended both
Men / into one man / with a man-sized growth.'"

He pauses. Smiles. Looks up from the book.
"That's from a piece by Drew. 'what zuber took
From us.'" He cradles it like it's a child.
His smile fades. "But Drew got reckless. Wild.
He felt he *was* The Mountain. If, in fact,
Hal Hawks was gone—and if you then subtract
The other two—who's left? James Gordon, lost

In time. And Drew." More B-roll. Dry leaves, frost-
Tipped blades of grass, and pages of a vintage
Calendar, perused by wind.

* * *

New footage:
Drew is at a harpsichord, positioned
In a barren desert. "Drew commissioned
Me"—still Hashtag's voice—"to film and spread
His long-awaited version of 'The Dead,'
As *he* imagined it, based solely on
The MOJO essay. It was close to dawn,
And Drew had finally found the perfect spot."

A map fades in—the Gobi, marked with dot—
Then back to Drew. His t-shirt, once a gleaming
White, is grey. He's nodded off or dreaming,
Head down, eyes shut, hands upon the keys.
His jeans are torn, the rips disgorging knees.
At Drew's feet, kneeling followers await
The start. He looks as if he's lost some weight.

And then he plays some chords that sound both odd
And somehow right, as if unlocked by God
And found by fingers for the first time ever.
He starts to list the names of bands that never
Made it big, and goes beyond the ones
The MOJO essay quotes: "The Only Ones!
The Cramps!" He cries, "And here's where all the strings
Come in!" But no strings start to swell. He sings,
"And now the children's choir!" But no more voices

Join. It's only Drew—and yet, it's joyous.

Suddenly, the song drops off, sounds under-
Water. Squeaky. "Sorry, stupid blunder,"
Hashtag says. "Forgot I was recording.
Scratched my ear."

* * *

                  Dissolve to people boarding
Someone's giant pleasure yacht, a pass
Around each person's neck: a square of glass
That's H-shaped. Some are waving, others holding
Up their Hs. One man, arms enfolding
Wife or girlfriend, shuffles forward as
The line slinks up the gangway, buoyant jazz
Tromboning from the deck, where several horns
Provide a welcome. Zoom in. Gold adorns
Each horn's lapel: an H-shaped pin. Beside
The pickup band—the drone shot going wide—
A man in light-grey suit, his face behind
A surgical mask.
                 "You have to keep in mind"—
Cut back to Gates—"how big, how *huge*, a deal
This was." He shows an envelope, its seal,
An "H" in wax. Dissolve to cursive—"*You
Plus One Are Formally Invited To*"—
Then back to Gates. "The invite, to the most
Exclusive party ever, came by post.
An actual human hand-delivered every
One."
        The film now cuts to men in reverie
On the yacht's broad deck, a champagne flute

In each one's hand. We see some plattered fruit
Beneath a swarm of bonsai gulls, self-chilling
Sculptures made of ice, and people milling.
A blood-red sun, projected by computer
From Mount Fuji's peak, lies on the pewter
Cloud, indifferent to its flow. (Japan
Projects assorted prefab suns that span
The rainbow. Red implies the dusk.)

                                    "This guy,"
Says Gates, "one Edmund H, had worked to buy
Up all the copies of *The Dead*—then kept
Them to himself. So Mountain fans, like, wept
When Edmund finally decided he
Would play one. A- and B-side. Mountain Tea
Would now be heard again. Apparently,
The guy had done extensive therapy
About his inability to play
His mint and near-mint discs. He'd tried to slay
His demons."

                    Drone's-eye view of H's yacht
Zooms in and slowly pans across a plot
Of pedestals: short columns domed with glass,
Which span a makeshift stage. "He sent the pass,"
Says Gates, "to critics, fans, The Avian Flu's
Ex-members, Drew—and took us on a cruise.
The invite said he'd play the songs at sea.
He'd finally let the world hear Mountain Tea."
On each short pedestal (the footage choppy
Due to waves) there lies a single copy
Of *The Dead*. Its bedding is a half-
Shell, scalloped. No one—this includes the staff
Employed by H for decades—is allowed

To touch the glassed-in singles. Soon a crowd
Is waiting by the stage. Up near the front
Stands Drew, with Jesus beard. "Look, I'll be blunt,"
Says Gates. "The guy looked haggard."

                                  Alice. "No,
I didn't go." She smiles. "I had a show.
My first since leaving Drew. I hadn't seen
Him in, like, months. I figured they would screen
The big reveal on ZuckTube. Anyway,
I didn't love The Mountain. Loved to play
Is all. Life's short."

                 Cut back to H's yacht,
The man himself up on the stage, a bot
Beside him, man-sized but without a pilot—
The sort of model that can thread an eyelet,
On a sail, with cordage, or spot stars
To steer by, or tend main-deck tiki bars,
Or tie assorted sailor's knots, or speak
When spoken to. It's made of oiled teak
And sports a blue-and-white-striped naval shirt,
Plus white capris. It seems to be inert.
Higashi's clearly speaking, but the voice
Of Gates breaks over.

                "H had made a choice,
He told the crowd, to change his life. He'd drowned
His old self in the sea. He said he'd found
So many new and lovely friends that day."
As Gates voiceovers, H begins to sway,
A little tipsy. H had been expected
To maintain a business he'd rejected
In his heart, a family business handed
Down to him. He often felt quite stranded,

On his own. He said he had one friend,
A man named Jennings, and he liked to spend
His time collecting things. He had no wife.
The Mountain Tea—his phrasing!—was his life.
He'd learned to only love things that were mint
Or rare or, even better, out of print.
He liked to write, and talked about a book
In progress. "Maybe one of you would look
It over for me." H got quiet there.
His head was bowed. He seemed to be in prayer.

"And then," continues Gates, "H sighed and said,
'I should've done this sooner. Here's *The Dead*.
I'll see you on the other side'." With that,
H steps up to·a pedestal—the gnat-
Like bonsai gulls above—and reaches *through*
The dome of liquid glass, a special brew
That reads his DNA and ripples slightly.
(Blowfish needles swell up when the nightly
Cleaning staff on H's yacht brush by
The liquid glass. These see-through quills will fly
And pierce intruders.)
                              H picks up the sleeve,
Removes its record as you might retrieve
A baby from its incubator, each
Arm risking guillotine. But there's no breach;
The glass accepts him. H, of course, decides
To leave the sleeve inside the dome. The tide's
Been growing, and he doesn't want to risk
The threat of sea spray. Next, he brings the disc
Back through the dome, which makes a sucking burp
As it reseals. The only sound: the slurp

And slap of waves.
On cue, the bot tugs back
Its hood-like hair and pulls its face down, slack,
Around its neck—a scarf of skin. It catches
Sun, the skull, and sparkles. H unlatches
Something and, his fingers spread, unscrews
The skullcap of the bot. Assorted "oohs"
And "ahs." This leaves the lower half, sub-brow,
A flat-topped plain. The skull, thus scalped, is now
In playing mode.
Cut to crowd shots: people
Clapping, one man crying, hands a steeple
Propping chin. (His glasses float before
His eyes.) The yacht is very far from shore.

With utmost care, H sets the disc above
The skull. Peels off a hand (he's had a glove
On). Flying-saucer-like, the record floats,
Midair.
Gates lifts his claws and makes air quotes.
"'The tragic loss of life that day was *not*
My client's fault. It was the faulty bot.'
Drew's lawyer's statement . . ."
Cut to Hashtag Blessed.
"Yes, Drew and I were there, but to the best
Of my"—cough—"knowledge, Drew had no part in
What happened."
H's disc begins to spin
Above the scalped head, which is needleless.
The bot's mouth, wide, begins to stream a hissing
Sound. The bot then lifts its hands to still
The disc—which screeches as a record will

When scratched by DJ hands. Its fingers grip
The disc (the crowd confused) and duly rip
The thing in two.

                Quick cut to Gates. "And then
The bot went nuts. It plucked a fountain pen
From H's suit's breast pocket and it started
Stabbing him. H fell. And then it darted
To the pedestals and started smashing
Glass. At this point, everyone was crashing
Into one another, freaking out.
The pedestals, in self-defense, were sprouting
Spiny, foot-long quills. These started shooting
Through the air." The bot, a blur, is rooting
Through a writhing dome, to seize and tear
Apart another precious disc. "That's where
It died," says Gates. "The dream. And when the final
Disc was shards, the bot curled up, its spinal
Column rigid"—finely furred with quills,
The bot appears in several drone's-eye stills,
In fetal OFF mode—"sleeping." Gates breaks off.

"No *way* did Drew have any hand in"—cough,
  Cough—"smashing all those discs," says Hashtag Blessed.
He folds his arms. Stares at the camera.
                     West.
"But if a man were trying to be Mountain
  Tea, he'd *want* a bot to take a fountain
  Pen and stab to death the man who'd hoarded
All those discs. MacLeod had just recorded
His take on 'The Dead.' He planned to do
The B-side, 'Yesterday,' as well. The Flu
Would be irrelevant if suddenly

The world could hear the songs of Mountain Tea.
The Flu existed *to* dream up lost work."

"How does a bot," says Gates, "like, go berserk,
But somehow only kill a single man,
And only smash his discs? It was a plan —
That's what some say. One rumour is that Drew
Had found a backer. Wealthy guy who threw
A ton of cash his way. That's how he financed
It." Dissolve to H's body, eye lanced
By a pen. Two off-screen men now black
Out H with sheets. "The only way to hack
A rich guy's bot." Around the corpse are scattered
Ink-dipped flower petals: shards of shattered
Vinyl. Beneath the sheets, the pen's produced
A single peak. "Well, that's what some deduced.
Who knows? But later, someone did post to
The *Knot* a screen grab of a cheque for Drew —
From 'J.G. Inc.'" Gates lifts his shaggy brows.

* * *

Exterior shot of nightclub, several scows
Outside. Interior shot of stage, a single
Stool and mic. A couple people mingle,
Holding pints or staring into space —
At postcards? Alice X straps on her bass
And takes the stage. The camera pans around,
Revealing several dozen fans. The sound
Is slightly muffled, likely bootlegged from
Smartears. But Alice X begins to hum
A melody, and with a pick begins
To play it. Soon she's singing of her sins,

Of waiting on a scow that keeps her dead
Beloved's corpse. Salvation's just ahead,
She wails, the words as ancient as the blues.
By next week, she will have ten million views
Onzuck. For now, she simply wants to play.
She calls the song "Another Yesterday."

The bonsai mountain goats had multiplied.
Three dozen specimens now occupied
The shelves and nooks in Edmund's library.
As Jennings walked, he scanned the carpet, wary
Of the toy-scale goats that sprang away
At every step. At times, the goats would bray
Or stand on stacks of unshelved books, which formed
A knee-high mountain range. The young ones swarmed
Him when he kneeled to leave a tray of grass
Supplied by Gardener. Sometimes Maid would pass
A vacuum through and hoover all their droppings.
Goats would flee to low, remote outcroppings—
Books in piles on the floor—or hide
Behind the brocade curtains.
                                          Jennings eyed
A black box on the desk where Edmund used
To work. Beside it, pages. "Elves unloosed
Their arrows at the orc," the top page read.
He flipped back to the cover sheet. *The Dead
Elf's Song*, by Edmund H. It was about
A troupe of singing elves who face a drought
Created by an evil wizard's spell
And fight assorted trolls dispatched from hell.

(They string their magic lutes like bows, and fire
Arrows at their foes.) The funeral pyre
Scene—where Gordyn, lead elf, lays his friend
Haldir to rest—would have to be the end,
Though; Edmund, dead for three whole years, had left
The work unfinished. (Still, the thing had heft;
He'd gotten almost up to page one thousand.)

Jennings put the sheets down. Outside, scows and
Cars whined by. The neighbour's green-skinned pup
Went "ribbit ribbit." Jennings, gloved, picked up
The small black box. Some kanji—etched upon
The lid, but moving, as if being drawn
Clean through the wood—composed a chyron parting
Fibres, the wood a strain of live, self-carving
Pine. They reached the edge and then turned back,
Like vintage vectors changing course on black
Computer screens.
                            The butler backtracked from
The room, the box in hand. He passed the glum
And bearded men who glowered out from frames
Along the hallway: patriarchs whose names
Began with "E" and ended with "Higashi."
Edmund's portrait—maskless, face an ashy
Hue—hung at the hallway's very end,
Right where the wall ran out. Around the bend
The wall resumed, but since Higashi's line
Had ended, Jennings had strung up some twine
And clipped on tintypes of the goats. (He only
Said he didn't like them; it got lonely
In the house when Gardener, Maid, and Cook
Were off on errands. So, he sometimes took

A shot or two.)
                      This four-skull skeleton crew
Had kept up Edmund's house, while lawyers, who
Were in no special hurry, sorted assets
From afar. The will had many facets—
Books, collectibles, a giant yacht,
A populated, bonsai Camelot,
And every kind of life-sized Manga statue,
Saucer-eyed and carved from resin, that you
Could collect.
                      He turned into the study,
Where the man in dark-grey tweed and muddy
Boots was sitting. Haze (the lawyers called
Him that) was signing papers that were sprawled
Across a table. Jennings gently placed
The live pine box before him. Haze (who faced
A yawning fireplace, in which some bonsai
Goats had made a nest) was speaking.
                                                    "On my
Life," he said. "The butler's brought the box
In. *The* box. Send." He seemed to be in talks
With someone via postcard.
                                        Jennings took
A small step back, but couldn't help but look
As Haze, deep breath, placed one hand on the lid.
The kanji text, ping-ponging, paused—then slid
Back to the centre. Jennings knew it said,
Translated, "MT Box: Remains of Dead."

Haze flipped the lid. The red glare of the sun-
Light streaming through the dusty study's one
Uncurtained window—prefab dusk, projected

Clear across Roppongi—caught selected
Shards of something shiny, black, and thin.
"Reply to Gibs," said Haze, who wore a grin.
"They're here." He held a piece up to the light
And turned it slightly as a jeweller might
A gemstone. "Send." The shard was whorled with grooves.

Jennings jerked the way a puppet moves
When yanked from rest. His mouth began to speak
In someone else's voice. "You have a week,"
He heard himself intone. "The will is crystal
Clear." (Higashi's lawyers, based in Bristol,
Worked through Jennings when they couldn't make
The trip to Tokyo; they wouldn't take
A Zuber booth.) "Our client wanted you
To have a chance to hear the discs. He knew
How much they meant to you. He never thought
They'd be like *this*, of course. Perhaps a bot
Can fix them? Anyway, please send a post-
Card if you have a question." As a ghost-
Flush form will slump because its spirit's fled,
The butler's body slackened slightly, head
Tipped forward. Then, the head snapped up, the mind
Of Jennings back in charge.
                                        Haze had signed
The last release. The butler noted that
The man's John Hancock, formed by several fat
And ragged loops of ink, betrayed a lack
Of skill in cursive. Men these days had slack
And sloppy manners, Jennings thought. A shame.
He noted that the man had spelled his name
With "y," not "z."

Hayes stood, the box in hand,
And turned to Jennings. Jennings bowed and fanned
An arm out: this way. At the front door, Hayes
Looked back.
                    "We'll see you here in seven days,"
Said Jennings, glove on doorframe. Hayes allowed
A nod and turned to exit. Jennings bowed
Again and closed the door.

* * *

                        When Hayes looked back,
The townhome—wedged between Espresso Hack,
A boutique roastery, and Burberry—
Was gone, as if excised by surgery.
The ground, an open hole, was fenced in by
A gate, which Hayes had just clicked shut. "Reply
To Gibs," he said. He looked up at the under-
Sides of passing scows and hailed one.

* * *

                            Thunder
Rumbled through the quiet Rosedale street.
The space between two townhomes swirled with sleet
As if a mini-rainstorm had invaded
The vacant lot. A third home slowly faded
In between the other two, its limestone
Bricks resolving in the brand-new time zone.

The front door opened. Jennings popped his bald
Head out; the townhome had indeed installed
Itself back where its brickwork sat most days:
Toronto, EDT. That fellow Hayes

Was still in Tokyo, still waiting for
His scow to land.
                              The butler closed the door
Behind him, placed a bowler on his head,
And headed out to buy a loaf of bread.
The house saw very little in the way
Of guests. Still, Jennings started every day
(The day had started over; it was morning
In Toronto) buying bread.

* * *

                              "Still mourning
Master, eh?" the tech girl'd said a few
Months back, when Gardener, worried that a screw
Was loose inside his colleague's skull, brought in
Some help. She'd peeled down Jennings's mask-like skin
And taken off his skullcap. Next, she'd spread
Both lobes. The bot knew Edmund had been dead
Three years. And yet: he'd go buy bread or draw
A bath or pour a Coke (a bendy straw
Placed like a periscope) and leave the drink
On Edmund's writing desk, the shifting ink
On spines the only movement. All the bots
Had been inspected for unhealthy thoughts
Three years before, just after Edmund's "passing,"
Quote unquote. They'd all endured trespassing
Thumbs among their thoughts.
                              Gardener stood
Off to the side, arms folded. "Should be good,"
The tech girl said to Gardener as she tightened
Something. "There." The butler's eyes had brightened
Slightly. And for several days, the butler

Seemed all right. He started back on clutter,
Bagging Edmund's things. Took tea with Cook
And Maid and Gardener.
                              Soon he found a book,
Though, lying on the ground, half-eaten by
The goats. And Jennings, with a wary eye
Behind him, slipped the work of poetry
Inside his jacket. It was *Mountain Tea*,
By Peter Van Toorn. His master used to read
The book aloud while sitting up in bed,
And Jennings, passing in the hall, would pause
To listen. Edmund's style had its flaws;
He really didn't read a lot of verse
Except for Tolkien, so his voice got terse
And underscored the rhymes. Like many lost
In loving Gordon's band—who hadn't glossed
A poem since grade twelve—he'd sourced and bought
The Véhicule edition. Edmund thought
That every fan of Gordon's band should know it.

But soon he'd come to love Van Toorn, a poet
From Montréal. And Jennings, as he idled
Outside Edmund's bedroom, found the wild
Poems—hollered by an amateur
Who hadn't read much verse and felt unsure;
Who stomped the rhymes like someone in a waltz—
To be as stirring as the smelling salts
A butler, worth his salt, is armed with. (Mellow
Verse—fine British fellows like Longfellow—
That's what Jennings had been versed in.)
                                                    Plus,
It seemed like Edmund made such noisy fuss

When looking for his *Mountain Tea* because
He liked to draw the butler near, the buzz
Of Jennings's joints a comfort. Book recovered,
He'd shoo the bot away. But Jennings hovered
In the hall; that's what he sensed his master
Wanted, iambs pulsing through the plaster:
"Shake off the crazies! Sober up, Li Po!"
Hard stress on "Po!"

               The butler's room—below
The townhome's ground floor, where the servants slept—
Had one chair and a bureau. Jennings stepped
Inside. He held the book a beat, then stored
It in the bureau.

             Soon he had a hoard
Of Edmund's things—so many things they spilled
Out on the floor. (He'd broken Butler's Guild
Rule One: Don't Pinch.) A first edition of
The Hobbit, which his master, with a glove,
Had only ever handled once; a floppy
Disc once owned by Something Jobs; a copy,
Signed by author, of *The Diamond Age*;
A monk-made, vellum *Beowulf*; a page
Of writing in the hand of Alan Moore;
A puck-sized tchotchke that, placed on the floor,
Would grow a life-sized selfie (Edmund, posed
With hand-drawn Lara Croft, who'd been transposed
Upon the holo by some trick of tech);
A rare, complete, and mint condition deck
Of *Magic* cards from 2035
On pixiepaper (trolls would come alive
And cry and swing their axes when you placed
A card down in the heat of play); encased

In packaging, assorted statuettes
Of female Manga types (their heavy chests
And sculpted asses bulged as if a hand
Had squeezed their torsos, leaving waistlines sand
Could trickle through).

                    So when he slept at night—
The butler standing upright until light
Lit up the square of smartpaint representing
Windowpane—he'd feel the unrelenting
Loneliness relent a little bit.
And when the smartpaint, synched to morning, lit
The butler's face—and when his eyelids slowly
Opened onto Edmund's stuff—a holy
Feeling filled the room and seemed to hover
By his ear. The butler, then, would cover
Up the stash with sheets. He'd leave and lock
His door. And smile.

*   *   *

                    Jennings liked to walk
Along the tree-lined Rosedale street. The maples—
Knotty, bulbous—were like trees in fables.
Because the growing Cloud had blocked the sun,
Most major Western cities had begun
To use a steroid in their drinking water.
The greenery that once appeared to totter
On the edge of death began to bloom
Again—with stubborn force. A hydra plume
Of bulbs would sprout where one bulb was the norm.
A shoot would swell and take the sprawling form
Of knotty, sprite-infested bark in prose tales
From the past. The roadside trees in Rosedale

Reached above the road and laced their leaves
Together. Some had even reached the eaves
That caught the rain and ran across the tony
Mansion tops, and with a brutish, stony
Coolness—that of weather, say, or time—
Had splayed and spread and, vine-like, slowly climbed
The roofs. It looked like maples had disgorged
The pricey homes; like brickwork had been forged
In tree bark.
        Several servant bots were sitting
On a curb, heads lowered. Flies were flitting
Round their faces. But the bots, at rest,
Stayed still, their knees tucked to their naked chests,
Their fingers knit. Beside their feet, their shoes
Stood, as if worn by spirits. Bots with screws
Loose were abandoned sometimes. Homes were sold,
Estates carved into parts, and all the old
Appliances placed roadside. It was cheaper
To turn loose a bot and start "grim reaper"
Mode than change their programming to meet
The needs of some new master. Thus the street
Was destiny. The servant's brain would fill
With strange, unbidden thoughts. They'd walk until
They reached their house's curb, then duly strip,
Sit down, and wait. A Zuber truck would ship
Them up to heaven.
        There were empty lots
Between some houses. People who owned plots
Around the globe would move their homes among
The different properties. Higashi's swung
Between Toronto and Roppongi several
Times a month. The townhome, like a vessel,

Shipped its molecules by way of Kite,
A Zuber service that dissolved from sight—
And reassembled elsewhere—domiciles
Of all kinds. (A ZuckTube ad showed tiles
On a kitchen floor beginning to swirl,
The chessboard pattern spinning like a whirl-
Pool, forming, funnel-like, a throat down which
The oven, table, chairs, and other kitchen
Items slid, the house collapsing in
Around a point. The point then grew a thin
Line, which began to trace a diamond shape:
A kite.)
           The homes gave way to shops. A crêpe
Stand, mailbox-sized and poised upon a post,
Unshuttered and produced, as if a ghost
Were coiled inside, a hand that held a paper
Cup. A well-dressed man received it, vapour
Rising off the coffee. Then, the hand
(Whose owner was across the world and manned
The kitchen in a shop in Harajuku)
Drew back in the modest box, withdrew to
Where it came from.
                Takeout boxes lined
The sidewalks, customers at each one, blind
To what was on the other end, a holo
Menu floating overhead. You'd swallow,
Cough, and say your order. Then, a man
Or woman at the crêpe place in Japan
Would hear the order and get down to work.
(The customer would have to sort of lurk
About.) The server—both across the world
And not, like one edge of a map that's curled

In on itself—would pass the order through
A square of light. Their arms would form anew
In Rosedale; each would quickly reassemble,
Inch by inch, and perfectly resemble
Its original, extending from
The box. The order didn't drop; each thumb,
Far from its brain, still heard its brain's commands
And held the crêpe or coffee 'til new hands,
The customer's, took over. Then, the limbs
Withdrew (until another set of whims
Appeared).

        You *could* just beam the order by
Itself, of course. But steak-and-kidney pie
Sold better when presented by a pair
Of English arms. And slow-cooked wild hare
Seemed more authentic if a French chef's fingers
Passed it to you. Something soul-like lingers
On real skin—or anyway, that's what
The surveys said. The servers' arms should jut
From boxes.

        Jennings spoke his order to
An ornate grille, the window to Mon Chou,
A shop in Paris. (Horns—some jazz quartet's—
Piped through a speaker.) Soon, two long baguettes
In paper sleeves emerged, and at the end,
The hands that held them. With the briefest bend
Of torso—Jennings always bowed—he headed
Off, baguettes in hand. The box then shredded
Each hand back to atoms, as the hands
Retracted.

        Jennings paused at other stands.
He said the names of cheeses Edmund loved,

And waited. (Dark-skinned fingers, these ones gloved,
Emerged with several squares of cheese in wax.)
He stopped to watch a busker play her sax.
He had no way of knowing yet that Hayes,
Mere beats ago, had perished in a blaze.
The rusted scow he'd hailed had taken off,
But soon began to shudder, clank, and cough
Out smoke. It lost its thrusters and began
To plummet. Nothing would be salvaged—man
Nor driver nor the box that Hayes had held.
The vinyl fragments of *The Dead* had melded.

Jennings nodded at a passing bot
And paused before another box, Grape Scott!,
And named a wine that Edmund liked to serve.
The wine emerged. The butler's optic nerve,
Which had a chip by Interac, conveyed
A string of digits to each box. (He paid
By glance.)
                    At home, the butler made a plate
Of cheese, baguette, and wine, and brought it straight
To Edmund's bedroom door. He left it on
The floor and knocked.
                              He found the plate at dawn,
Surrounded by assorted bonsai goats.
He shooed them off and left a bowl of oats,
And deftly bussed the other plate away.
The butler did this every single day.

* * *

A couple weeks went by, the townhome shifting
Back and forth between its cities, lifting

Dust and brittle leaves up in its wake.
November had arrived. The house would take
Its winter in Saint Kitts, its bricks displaced
To pricey, sunbathed property that faced
The sea.
                    One morning, out among the shops,
The butler saw a crowd had formed. Two cops
Arrived and pushed their way through. Jennings moved
In closer. Someone's severed arm—removed
Quite cleanly at the bicep—lay upon
The ground, below the box for Leaf and Fawn,
A tea stand. It was weird how smooth the stump
Was: like the cut a slicer makes in plump
Bologna.
                    Teleporting arms was fairly
Safe—as safe as driving. (Glitches rarely
Happened.) It felt as if you'd thrust your limb
In water; where it crossed the frame, a rim
Of tingling ringed your skin. And as you drew
Your limb back to some room in, say, Peru,
The rim slid off the arm—and off the hand—
Or so it seemed. In fact, your arm was sand
Right where it crossed the takeout window's frame,
And if the window froze, then you could maim
Yourself—just by withdrawing, quickly, one
Half of an arm the window wasn't done
Assembling.
                    Jennings heard the server's cries
Bleed through the box. In Rosedale, though: deep sighs.
"This happens every other week," a well-
Dressed man said to one cop. "And there's a smell.
It sticks around for days." A woman with

A Prada bag spoke up. "At least the fifth
Time someone's dropped an arm." The cop turned off
The box's cries, and made as if to doff
A non-existent hat. "Good day and please
Move on." The cries had sounded Cantonese
To Jennings.

        As the crowd dispersed, he stood
A moment longer. Jennings felt he should—
And this felt sort of odd—pray for the faceless
Owner of the arm, who lived a stateless
Life, between two worlds. The cop, however,
Gestured. "Move *on*." The arm the box had severed
Twitched a bit.

        A year from now, that group
Of white supremacists, The Ivory Troop,
Would storm Grape Scott!—the giant flagship one
In Rome—and seize control by threat of gun.
They'd lean through several dozen takeout windows,
Torsos crossing several dozen limbos.
One would bloom from Rosedale's mailbox, spraying
Bullets at pedestrians and slaying
Ten "elites," the word their leader, breathless,
Later used onzuck. (Of course, the death
Of kids, he would concede, had been unplanned.)

* * *

Jennings shuffled off, his bag in hand,
And headed home. But on arrival at
The house, he found a hole; the welcome mat
Announced a crater. Fencing had gone up
While Jennings had been out.

        The neighbour's pup—

Half-dog, half-frog—was in the next yard, chained
And hopping. "Coming Soon," a sign explained,
And Jennings knew that Edmund's house was gone
For good.
    Beyond the hole, the backyard's lawn
Lay freshly cut. Had Gardener somehow known
The plot was to be sold? A bat-sized drone
Was overhead, updating Zuck Maps's Street
View feature. Jennings heard a tiny bleat;
A bonsai goat was by his feet.
        He knew
His upper lip, bot-stiff, would see him through;
He also knew his mind would soon be wiped
Remotely. (Long ago, his death was typed
Into his system.) Once grim-reaper mode
Began, he'd lose control. A line of code
Would steer him to the curb. He'd stand and wait
To be collected by the truck. His fate,
Of course, was space; he knew that heaven was
A myth you tell to bots with vacuumed fuzz
For brains—a Roomba, say. Old bots were bound
And beamed off-world. They'd freeze and tumble sound-
Lessly inside the Cloud, trajectories
Adjusted by debris.
      The destinies
Of Gardener, Cook, and Maid remained unclear.
In fact, a day from now their brains would steer
Them to the sidewalk in Roppongi, where
The home had shifted, Jennings unaware.
They'd march like zombies to the curb and turn
To watch the fading home, a spirit, spurn
Them. (Edmund's quaint, well-kept Victorian

Would land in storage outside Edmonton.)
Junk mavens, pulling wagons, would collect
The roadside bots and, using saws, dissect
Them for spare pieces.

                             Jennings placed his fingers
On the fence. He knew a spirit lingers
Sometimes. Maybe Edmund's was around
Still. Maybe it had somehow held the ground
His home had failed to. Overhead, the trees
Were silent, branches meshed so tight the breeze,
A weak one, couldn't stir them. Jennings knew
The spirit had moved on.

                             The goat withdrew
As Jennings turned—then sniffed its way a little
Closer. At this point, Boy Scout bots would whittle
Something. Altar bots who clean cathedrals,
When discarded, prayed to stave off evil's
Influence. A yoga bot would sit
And form a lotus. Most would simply knit
Their hands, heads down.

                             Jennings was supposed
To prep himself for death: to man his post
And polish shoes. Most butlers were designed
To take their clothes off, fold them up, and mind
Society by sitting down, their knees
Pressed to their chest. Their CPUs would freeze.
Their limbs would lock.

                             Instead, he started saying
Lines from *Mountain Tea*. It looked like praying
To the well-dressed people walking by.
It was, he felt, the decent way to die.

8.

Cassie Kaye, staff zlogger for *The Slope*,
Which *Rolling Stone* had dubbed "the great white hope
Of Mountain criticism," stood and gazed
Across the beach. The oddity—a crazed
Shape writhing underneath a dark-grey sheet,
Like tendrils draped in cloth—was several feet
Above the ground. A large crowd stood around
It, pointing, laughing. It was vaguely round,
The thing, and had drawn several Zuckgram selfies.
Cassie, though, had hung back on her shelf
Of sand. She brought a thumb up to her lips:
A thumb's-up sign—or so it seemed.
                                        "Low ships,
Far off, inch by," she said to thumb. "A crowd
Has formed. The sky is more or less the Cloud,
The perfect backdrop to unveil, well, what
It is, who knows? Please print."
                                        Those two words cut
The sentence off and sent it into space,
Towards a head-shaped satellite (its face
The face of Zuck himself), which duly sent
The sentence back to Earth. The sentence bent
Towards assorted laptops, smarteyes, wrist-

Based difference engines, zPads, and the cyst-
Sized hard drives in some brains—all in a blink.

It was the latest post for Those Who Think,
The shorthand Cam had started using when
Describing readers of *The Slope*: the men
(Just men) who wanted more than glorified
Fan fiction, which is what the *Knot* supplied;
The men who wanted rumour-mongering.

She headed down the dune. She wore a sling
Across her light-grey camisole, a weathered
Pouch she kept her hand on. Short hair, feathered
At the ends, had lost its shape—that's what
The hotel mirror said. "Time for a cut!"
It chirped. She wondered if, much like her mother,
It had other cutting thoughts on other
Things: her vintage tatts; her military
Shorts.
      She walked a little closer, wary
Of the man who also hovered just
Outside the crowd. His silver hair was mussed.
His glasses, floating ones, were dark, as was
His suit—a fuck-you to the heat? The buzz
Onzuck was that the founder of the *Knot*
(*The Slope*'s sworn enemy, or so Cam thought)
Was mourning. Clearly, though, he wasn't so
Distraught he couldn't make the trip and show
His face at The Unveiling. Cassie raised
Her thumb.
        "The thing beneath the sheet, a crazed

Shape, writhing up above, but out of sight,
Is mesmerizing: frozen in midflight
And just within the grasp of all the fans
Who've made it out. Please print." A couple pans
("Zoom in, snap that, please print") and what her eyes
Had taken in—the sand, the crowd, the sky's
Grey slate—appeared upon *The Slope*'s live zlog.

"Hello."

        She looked down. Small boy. With a frog
Tee. Dark hair. Shorts. She stared at him, her thumb
Still raised.

        "Hello," she said, and then, "The sum
Of Mountain knowledge seems to be out on
The sand." Her eyes still on the boy. "The dawn
Is giving way to morning. Soon we'll see
What some are saying will be poetry
In motion. Print." (She knew what Cam would say:
"Too purple, Cass. No poetry, okay?
Let's keep it clean.")

        The boy, his toes in sand,
His feet half-buried, squinted at her hand.

"That's cool," he said. Her thumb's nail wore a lacquer,
Revlon's DropMic, which some asshole hacker
Once broke into, stealing several hours
Of dictation—"call mom," "pick up flowers"—
And her passwords; pamphlets quickly swarmed
Her Zwitter page and left her pic deformed.
The hacker placed her head upon a porn
Star's neck, and filled her feed with zweets by born-

Again disgruntled gamers, reenactors
Of the Civil War, and anti-vaxxers.
Because it chipped, she touched the nail up twice
A month.
            "I know," she said, "it's pretty nice."

"Does it play games?" he said.
                            She smiled. "No."
She kneeled. "It's mostly just for writing."
                                    "Oh,"
He said, and looked away. The frog's neck bulged.
The little one she hadn't yet divulged
To Cam (their boy—or girl) would wear organic,
She decided then; and then the panic
Flooded in again. The latest pee
Test with a plus sign—pee test number three—
Was in the pouch she couldn't help but keep
A hand on (even when she'd tried to sleep
Last night). She quickly touched her stomach. She'd
Been doing this all day, a kneejerk need
That made no sense, this being, what, week four?

* * *

The man with silver hair stood by the shore,
His eyes at sea. "That Gibson?" Cam asked, in
Her ear. Cam saw what she saw, from Berlin;
She'd opened up her eye-view once she'd hit
The beach. "That's him," she said, and wondered, shit,
Had she in fact killed access to her eyes
Once Cam was done, last night?
                            She'd stripped, her thighs
In lace, and looked back at the floor-to-ceiling

Mirror in her suite's large bathroom, kneeling
How Cam liked, ass out. (She'd really tried
To say, "I'm tired"; she hated being eyed,
To think of Cam and how he liked to watch
Her, one hand on his keyboard, one, his crotch.
Her neck got tired, staring back, but Cam
Would cry, "Eyes on the mirror, Cassie, damn
It!," pissed off at the fickle proxy of
Her gaze.) At last, Cam's voice exploded—"Love
You, fuck!"—a shard of treble, followed by
His grunting. Cam had come. She'd turned off eye-
View seconds later—"Pupils off"—and made
Note of the beep. Then took the test and prayed
For negative. He hadn't seen her take
It—she was certain. Still, she had to make
Herself remember. What a rush of fear,
Like leaving on the stove.
                                            Inside her ear,
Cam coughed. "You think we need the shot?" he asked,
His "we" the sneaky way Cam often masked
An order.
                    "No." She watched the man kick sand.
"He's sad about his friend." The upper hand,
Of course, was Cam's; as editor, he'd over-
Ride her if need be. He liked to hover
When he had a writer on the ground.
He liked to hover over her. She found
It hard, Cam's presence. That said, it was rare,
The Slope dispatching journalists to stare
At something like the thing beneath the sheet;
There often wasn't Mountain news to zweet
Or zlog about.

          "Okay," said Cam, "just keep
It clean. No poetry." Her ear went beep.

"Who's sad?" the boy asked, staring at the ocean.
The sheet-draped object, still in thrashing motion,
Hadn't drawn his gaze. She held her squat
And looked out at the ocean, too. A yacht
Was inching by.
                    "Is mom or dad around?"
She asked. Who'd left this boy on sacred ground?
This was the beach, of course, where Byrne and Reid
(Their real names never caught on) had agreed
To meet. The legend went: the two had planned
To rendezvous and try to form a band
Again. The former bandmates hadn't seen
Each other in two decades. It had been
Too hard; they'd each left Montréal and gotten
Jobs and spouses. Neither had forgotten,
Though, the time they'd spent in Mountain Tea.
Retired, living in the States, they re-
Connected via Zuckbook. Soon, they'd made
A date to meet. But fate would make a braid
Of Byrne and Reid, and knot their Zuber streams
When both men beamed down on the beach. The dreams
Their minds held, dreams to reunite, entwined
As brainpans meshed to form a single mind.
And now, years later, someone had ignited
Interest in the legend and invited
Fans out to the beach, where, Christ, some bone-
Head had left Lovely Frog Boy on his own.

The crowd had grown to several hundred fans

In beachwear: shorts and hats and sockless Vans.
The small boy pointed.
                    "Dad is over there.
We're here for Grandpa. Dad said this is where
He died."
                She looked confused. "He died right here?"

He nodded. Cassie brought her thumb up near
Her chin, reflexively. "What was his name?"
The boy said, "Hugh McPhee. Let's play a game,
Okay?"
            Cam's voice squawked in her ear. "McPhee!"
He'd logged back in. "That's Reid! From Mountain Tea!"

* * *

A murmur rippled through the crowd. Two men
Were walking down the beach, in cloaks, and when
They reached the crowd, it parted. One man seemed
To lean upon his friend; his long hair streamed
Straight down, his fluffed-up beard afloat the way
A tulle skirt moves. The friend, who wore a grey
Scarf round his neck, held out an arm as if
To shield his charge, whose movements—shaky, stiff—
Were zombie-like.
                    "It's Drew!" a voice cried out.
Drew slowly raised an arm; it was about
The width of bone. His scarfed friend—Cassie knew
That this was Hashtag Blessed, one of a few
Men in the inner circle of MacLeod—
Steered Drew towards the floating thing. The crowd
Made "oohing" sounds as milk crates—like the kind
For storing records—beamed in and combined

To form a set of steps that led up to
The writhing, sheet-draped object.

Slowly, Drew
Climbed up the steps. He reached the top and faced
The crowd. The crowd began to clap. He placed
One hand upon the sheet and lifted up
The other; in its grasp, a golden cup
Materialized. (The bright, incoming item
Forced the raised and open hand to widen
Slightly.) Stuntman stuff: to aim shit at
A limb. She'd once seen someone beam a hat
Into another's skull, on ZuckTube, brim
Emerging *from* the brow. It was a grim
And viral clip—and brief; the pair of smart-
Eyes, filming, looked away. A dangerous sport,
But Drew was clearly quoting what had made
This beach so famous.

(Later, fans would trade
Their detailed theories, on the *Knot*, and she
Would read them: essays on the poetry
Of Drew's allusive gesture, dissertations
On his choice of cup, interpretations
Of the crates. She planned to read them all,
Replying secretly. It would appall
Cam, if he knew.)

Inside her ear, his voice
Was calm but firm. "We haven't got a choice,
Okay? We have to snap his face and post
The tintype. 'Grandson of Guitarist's Ghost.'
And then we need the parents."

Cassie shook
Her head. She moved in close to get a look

At Drew—"Snap that, please print"—and said, "I need
To zlog this, Cam. Let's talk about the Reid
Thing after."
                    Silence. "Cass, you have to keep
The kid in view."
                        Drew raised his voice. "I weep
When thinking of what happened on this beach
So many years ago. It's out of reach,
The music Byrne and Reid had planned to gift
The world. One might declare they sealed a rift
That day. But this 'collaboration' left
Their fans"—he touched his cup to chest—"bereft.
And yet there's hope that one day, yes, we'll find
James Gordon, Mountain Tea's true mastermind.
'Til then, my brilliant second-in-command,
My dear HB, has marked the great lost band
That nearly started in Fort Lauderdale,
Right here. His wrenching piece is called, 'A Tale
Of Two Men with One Heart.' We wanted you,
Dear friends and fans, to see it first."
                                        He drew
The sheet away. The shape appeared to be
In flux. (The invite *had* said, "poetry
In motion.") Cassie kept her head still so
She could record. It looked like two men flowing
Into one another, each one boring
Through the other's back like liquid pouring
In a loop: a moving figure eight
With arms and legs in tow, as grey as slate
But floating gently, just above the crowd.

Hashtag Blessed, who'd climbed the milk crates, bowed

As people clapped and cheered. Assorted bots
Beamed down. They wore bow ties, with polka dots,
And nothing else, their skin a creamy, plastic
White. They looked expensive—not the spastic
Bots you got from Hertz. Their groins were cod-
Piece smooth. A large turntable bot, the odd
Bot out, beamed in alone. It must've weighed
A ton. Its muscled flesh was solid jade,
Its feet were ornate paws. The rest held trays
With flutes of something fizzing.

                                        Cassie's gaze
Fell on the boy, off to the side and playing
In the sand. She wandered over, weighing
What to do. *The Slope* had been aggressive
In its mission. Cam had been obsessive
When it came to scooping Gibson's site.
But really, Cam had largely won the fight.
He'd post things no one else would touch: a tintype
Of Higashi, grainy, lying in
His coffin ("World Exclusive!") or explicit
Shots of Alice X ("All Nude—Don't Miss It!")
Purchased from an ex. But here, she had
To draw the line. The boy, alone, looked sad.
He'd drawn his own line in the sand, a line
Of pointy mountains.

                          "Cass!"—she arched her spine,
Cam's voice a shock—"he's drawing *mountains*. Snap
The shot."

              "Cam, look—"

                              "You need to cut the crap
And take the fucking tintype. Now." The boy
Looked up at her. Cam wanted to destroy

The *Knot*. A tintype of the grandson of
Lou Reid was ammunition. Up above,
The head of Zuck—below the Cloud, in space—
Awaited Cassie's jpeg of the face.

The boy said, "Want to play?" He couldn't hear
Cam's screaming—just a buzzing in her ear.

Drew and Hashtag stepped down on the beach.
Above, in flux, and floating out of reach,
The statue wove itself from man-shaped strands.
Drew went from fan to fan and touched their hands.

She touched her belly. "Pupils off," she said,
And hunkered down beside the boy. She spread
Her legs out in the sand. Her eyes were far
Away. The boy had drawn a five-point star
Above his mountain range. She drew a tree,
Her fingertip a pen. "I'm gonna be
A mom," she said.
                          He looked at her. "You hold
A baby this way, see"—his arms enfolding
Air. She laughed. And heard the popping sound.

A cry, the crowd's, rose up. She turned around.
The crowd, en masse, was running, blooming from
A single point: where Gibson stood, a gun
Wand up in Drew's astonished face. Its shaft
Was bright red. Set to lethal. Several craft—
The beach's lifeguards?—were already wheeling
Overhead. The drones were making squealing
Sounds, their bodies blinking: help.

                                    "You brought
That taxi down," said Gibson. "Had that bot
Kill Edmund."
                              On the ground, the rumpled form
Of Hashtag Blessed was still. Drew's face was warm,
Serene, eyes closed. He'd even opened up
His arms as if to hug his foe, his cup
Still in his hand.
                        A large man ran toward
The boy and scooped him up. (The dad?) The horde
Of Mountain fans, expanding out, had lost
Its shape. The waiter bots, well trained, had tossed
Their trays and crouched and interlaced their long
White fingers on their skulls. She heard a song
Begin to play.
                    Days later, when she played
Back what her eyes shot, Cassie saw the jade
Turntable bot. Back and forth, it wandered,
On the fritz, as Gibson, wand raised, pondered
What to do. A spinning halo—vinyl—
Spun above its flat-topped head. The final
Thing she got on tape before her gaze
Went black was Gibson screaming, "You killed Hayes!"
And then a light-pink mist replaced Drew's head.
The final sound: Drew's cover of "The Dead."

9.

From MOJO, June 2063.
Intro: "Cult Heroes: Felt to Mountain Tea."

The mythic footage RKO excised
From *Ambersons* remains as analyzed
As any vanished work of art—except
For Mountain Tea's *The Dead*. It's said Welles wept
Once, when the film was shown on television.
(The cut frames had been burned, a cruel decision
By the studio.) And yet at least
There *was* a film, if maimed, which got released
And can be seen a century later—botched
By editors at RKO, but watched
By countless numbers.
                              Mountain Tea, however,
Left few relics. Almost no one's ever
Heard its work. A couple documents
Exist, brief texts we treat as monuments:
The writings of a few reviewers back
In 2010 and (following a black-
Hole spanning decades) Patti Devin, in
These pages. But, to MOJO's great chagrin,
We never asked her for a copy of

The music she had found and come to love.
The files were destroyed—consumed by fire—
And Devin vanished.

                      But her words inspire
Us—inspired *me*. Yours truly was
A desperate English student, head abuzz
With thoughts of truth and beauty, when I found
Her poem. ("Essay" is too weak; it sounded
Like great verse, her reading of *The Dead*.)
We talked by zmail once—you've likely read
The transcripts. They remain a vital source
Of info on the band and changed the course
Of many lives. Some founded sites: the *Knot*,
The Slope. For my part, Devin's passion brought
Me here—away from grad school and towards
A life spent searching for the perfect words
To praise great music.

                      Devin's piece remains
Our most-read feature. Ever. With its strains
Of Marcus, Bangs, and Kael, her single page
Of text helped found a cult and set the stage
For music's greatest mystery: The Mountain.
That piece, reprinted next, provides the count-in
To a feature in the works for years,
Our guide to all the greats who reach few ears
But fire hearts—Chris Bell, The Sonics, Felt—
Cult heroes who have left a searing welt
Across our thoughts; whose records, hard to find
Or out of print, preoccupy our minds,
From Danny Whitten to The Avian Flu.
We search for vanished singers snatched by U-
FO (Jim Sullivan), great lives spent off

The grid (see Bobbie Gentry), those who scoff
At spotlights (Kevin Shields), and lost potential
(Drew MacLeod). Each entry is essential.

We like what Lawrence, Felt's late leader, said
In "All the People I like Are Those That Are Dead":

"All the people I like are in the ground.
It's better to be lost than to be found."

Our thoughts exactly.
                          And we have included
One new piece on rock's most veiled, occluded
Band. We sort out myth from mystery—
Involving ancient iPods, poetry
From Montréal (pre-Crater), businessmen
Who hoard rare art, a red-nibbed fountain pen,
A teleporter accident that spliced
Two bandmates' molecules (and duly sliced
The membership of Mountain Tea in half—
A Zuber mishap or a cosmic gaffe?),
The so-called "Bloody Sig," which some believe
Preserves James Gordon's plasma on its sleeve,
A monk who might be Hawks, a taxi scow's
Last fare. And melted vinyl.
                          As you browse
These pages, zweet at us and share your own
Cult heroes—those obsessions you alone
Love dearly. We believe in your belief.

—Hubert Ormsbie, Editor-in-Chief.

10.

Crater Books and Discs sat on the lip
Of Montréal's vast Crater, poised to tip
And plummet into semi-charted void.
The forty-year-old owner, Poe, employed
A two-man team: an English student, May,
Who spent the better part of every day
Providing play-by-play on feuds exploding
Zwitter-side; and Graham, who'd trained in coding
But, post-Crater, hadn't found a blip
Of work. The store, which claimed a narrow strip
Beside the chasm, was a freight container,
Retrofitted.
           May could not restrain
Herself when some poor fool brought in a book
By Rupi Kaur to sell or trade (a look
Of pain would seize her face). So Poe had placed
Her by the door, at cash. Her counter faced
Another, at the far end of the store,
Where Graham sat like a magistrate. He wore
A blank look (and a Slint tee) as he passed
Calm verdicts on the books and discs amassed
By sad men liquidating their collections,

Or grown men who'd outgrown their New Directions
Texts by Ezra Pound and cleared their basements.
Faced with gold, Graham kept his poker face.
Last week, he'd paid a couple bucks for *What's
The Matter Boy?* (Vic Godard) and The Ruts'
First single "Babylon's Burning." Both were now
Displayed behind the counter.

                                        "Take a bow!"
Poe cried out, once the sellers cleared the shop.
But Graham was mute, his shaggy '60s mop-
Top shining as he turned back to his MOJO.

Poe's denim jacket bore a "Back to Mono"
Button. His hair was grey. He worked the floor,
A long, two-sided bin, which spanned the store
And held the vinyl. Books and CDs lined
The walls. (Poe dealt in dumbprint and declined
To stock most smartbooks.) Silent men would stake
Their spots out, thumb through books, or, binward, make
Their way from "ADVERTS, THE" to "ZEVON, WARREN."
(Serge Gainsbourg, Afrobeat, and other "foreign"
Stuff was filed under all-consuming
"WORLD," which meant Non-English-Speaking.) Looming
Over shoulders, Poe would cheer on choices
("Ronnie Lane is great!") or not ("That's Joyce's
Arty shit. Try *Dubliners* instead.
The final story in the book, 'The Dead,'
That's art for sure, but readable as well,
You know?"). As Poe squeezed past his clientele,
He'd suck in gut. You had to press yourself
Against the bin, or flatten, flush with shelf,

To shop there.
                      But it was a quiet day,
The day the old man wandered in. "Which way,"
He asked, "is Schwartz's deli?"
                                May, her phone
In hand, stared at him. Ancient skin, but bone-
White bright, stood out against his dark-grey cloak.
Her phone let out a single, frog-like croak:
Bespoke alert from Zwitter. But her eyes
Stayed on him as the phone kept croaking. "Guys,
Which way is Schwartz's?"
                       Across the room, the two
Men, Poe and Graham, looked up. They'd been reviewing
Graham's most recent buys.
                    "A few rings down,"
Said Poe. The old man, though, was looking round.
Poe raised his voice a notch. "It's not this high,
Friend. Down the slope."
                  The old man loosed a sigh.
He pointed at a nearby shelf, whose piece
Of masking tape said, "POETRY." "MacNeice,"
He whispered. "*Springboard.*" Then he turned to look
At Poe and Graham. And smiled. "What a book!"
He turned back to the shelf.
                      Poe came around
The counter. Sidled over. "Yeah, I found
That one at an estate sale"—Poe looked back—
"A month ago?"
                The moptop, Beatle-black,
Nodded.
          "A month ago," said Poe.
                          The old

Man gently touched its spine.

        "You can, like, *hold*
It if you want," said Poe. He went to draw
The book out, but the old man laughed—"Haw!"—
And stilled Poe's hand.

       "That's kind, but no, my friend."
The spell had seemed to lift. "I must descend.
You said a few rings downslope, yes?"

          "About
That, yeah."

     The old man nodded, halfway out
The door. Then paused. He stood there, head cocked to
One shoulder. Seconds passed. "The music you
Have on," he said, "is that Hassid I'm hearing?"
"Josef Hassid?" He half-turned, one eye tearing
Slightly.

    Next to Graham, a full-sized, standing
Holo of a man, with MOJO branding
Overhead, was playing violin.
The man was young and colourless, his skin
Soft grey, as if he'd stepped free from a reel
Of ancient film. His movement wasn't real;
There were but a few surviving pics
Of him. (He died, Hassid, at twenty-six.)
A clever editor had animated
Them. The young man's brief career, truncated
By a mental illness, had become
A legend, and Hassid, a hero. Some
Now called Hassid the violin's Syd Barrett.

The old man stepped back in the store. "I swear it
Must be thirty years, the last time I

Heard 'Hebrew Melody'." He wiped his eye.

Poe looked at May who made a face like, "Um,
We're gonna *die* now."
                              Graham spoke up. "It's from
The latest MOJO, sir." He pointed at
The holo's shoes, which stood upon a mat,
Which was in fact an open magazine,
From which the man-sized holo—face serene,
Its right arm bowing—bloomed. The old man shook
His head.
                    "I used to buy that mag. They'd hook
You in each month by gluing on a free
CD." He looked at Poe. "A cheap degree
In music."
                    "We still like to stock it," Poe
Said. "*And* the mag still comes with music. No
CD, though. Holotunes."
                                        Hassid had reached
The end. His hair and suit went bright white, leached
Of grey tone, leaving but a silhouette,
Which soon began to fade. The mag reset
And flipped a page. A new form faded in
And filled with dabs of colour: Cocteau Twin
Liz Fraser. Frozen. Sound began to play.
Unfreezing, she began to slowly sway.

"We have that issue by the cash." Poe nodded
At May's counter. Unseen hands applauded;
Fraser, based on vintage footage from
An outdoor concert, now began to hum,
One hand on mic, eyes closed.

                              "No, no, I must
Be off," the old man said. He turned and, just
Like that, was out the door, Liz Fraser's head
Now wailing at the ceiling's lights instead
Of what it faced back when its keening cry
Was first put down on tape: a sun-filled sky.

* * *

At closing time, Poe locked up and then headed
To the Crater's edge. Small lights, embedded
In the darkness of the trench, implied
Their homes—a hundred thousand pods residing
On the Crater's walls and linked by spiral
Stairwells. This steel, corkscrewing, had a viral
Look from far away: long coils, climbing
Up and down the Crater's slopes and rhyming
With each other. Long ago—before
The missile fell—such stairwells linked the floors
Of Montréal's quaint walkups. Now, their coils,
Linked the many pods that bulged like boils
On the Crater's sloping sides.
                              Poe started
Down a stairwell, into dark. He'd charted
Out a longer path for walking home
Five weeks ago. He'd had more time to roam
Since Anne, his ex, had moved her few things out—
At least, that's what he'd told himself about
This recent tendency to take the long
Way back, or linger at the shop, a song
On repeat: "These Days," say, or "O My Soul."

The Crater was a massive, depthless bowl.

The bowl was lined with ridge-like rings, rock ledges
You could walk—assuming that the edges
Didn't spook you. Stairwells let you snake
Or ladder, up or down, at will, and make
Your way to different rings. Poe reached the third
Ring. Walked its curving path. He passed The Word,
His favourite bookstore, and a coffee stand.

"Small black," he said. A pasty girl who manned
The counter handed him a cup. He paid
With dumbcash—Zuckcoins didn't work—and made
It to another, twisting stairwell. Poe
Descended.
                Floating lanterns laid their glow
On sections of the spiral; otherwise,
It corkscrewed into darkness. Swarms of flies,
In spring, tornadoed in these lit-up spots.

He reached the fourth ring. There were public cots
Where winded folks could pause. He walked another
Arc of ring, and passed a pub, Queen Mother,
And assorted shops, each one a kind
Of cave carved into rock; each one behind
A thin and see-through wall of liquid glass,
A membrane made of hardly any mass,
Which rattled like tinfoil when a breeze
Kicked up. Instinctively, he touched the keys
Inside his pocket.
                People sidled past
Poe, trailing hands across the rock. A blast
Of wind could blow you off, so some observed
A careful distance from the edge, which curved

To match the wall. But Poe was cavalier
And took the outside lane. He'd lived down here
For years.
         The next few stairwells ran along-
Side vertical lines of pods. The sound a gong
Still makes five seconds after it's been banged
Was omnipresent as foot traffic clanged
Upon the countless steps: a drone the Crater
Multiplied. The world in Lynch's *Eraser-*
Head, Poe's favourite film, contained a drone
At times as well, a room tone all its own.
True works of art, Poe felt, were worlds that made
Their own strange sense. Their suns projected shade,
Their clouds rained light, their rivers arched like foaming
Bridges, following their authors' roaming
Whims.
         The pod-lined Crater was a kind
Of world as well, except no artist's mind
Had conjured it. The acting president,
Don Jr, ordered it by accident.
The tech behind the terra-missile, based
On Zuber's IP, basically displaced
The ground it targeted to space—and sculpted
Out a screw-shaped chasm. What resulted,
Ribbed with ledges, could be mined or later
Populated. But the navigator
Had some bugs; the terra-missile, meant
To terraform a tract of Arctic, bent
Towards a brand-new target: Montréal.
It later looked like God had mashed a ball
Into Québec; from space, a dark depression
Could be seen. This act of dispossession

Took twelve seconds, claiming homes, the earth
They stood on, poodles tied to parking meters,
Railways, buses, buildings, movie theatres,
Students at their laptops, men in reverie,
Lost and strolling with their Starbucks. Every
Form of life—from women giving birth
To blood-slick newborns—was delivered crying
Into outer space's vacuum, dying
Quickly.

        Those who made their lives beyond
The missile's radius were spared, but spawned
Mutations. Some woke up with scrambled parts.
One stone-still couple's chests had traded hearts.
The missile's fading reach erased some toes.
The remnants came to circle and enclose
The planet, merging with a cloud—the Cloud—
Of exostuff that humans had allowed
Themselves to Zuber out to outer space
In such great quantities they'd changed the face
Of Earth.

        Months passed. In time, the folks not killed,
Who lived near Montréal, climbed down and filled
The hole. It was the sort of premise art
Demands we trust—like when great stories start
With gambit: Gregor has become a fly,
Or screaming missiles falling from the sky
In London, World War Two, are correlated
With—or very possibly created
By—the hard-ons had by Pynchon's hero.

Poe headed down another flight. Ground Zero,
Far below the fiftieth ring, had not

Been walked on yet—or seen. Bot after bot
Had been deployed, sent down inside the chasm.
None returned. Some said that ectoplasm,
Pooled, had filled a basin at the bottom.
When bots passed, long tendrils rose and caught them—
Pulled them under. Others claimed pollutants
From the missile had created mutants
Living on the lowest rings. Their spines
Had sprouted tails, their tongues had forked. The mines
They'd tunnelled housed their young, and when a bot
Or Zuck Maps drone drew near, the mutants shot
The interloper with a spear and reeled
It in.
      Some felt the strange magnetic field
Projected by the Crater's walls had downed
These scouts. (Most Wi-Fi signals were confounded.)
So, the Crater's techie occupants
Had strung the rock with cable; steely glints,
Where cable had been stapled, winked like jewels.
In short, they'd spurned the Zuck and, winding spools
Around the stairwells, had contrived a closed
Web all their own.
      A protocol, imposed
By Crater chieftains, kept the many rings
Connected to the outside. Newsy things
Were captured by a bureau stationed on
The Crater's edge, which worked all night. At dawn,
It fed its copy through the web of cables
To arrive on screens at breakfast tables.
Pop-up pamphlets, with their talk of "Jews"
And "red pills," were avoided. Old-school news
Was vetted and delivered by a team

Of editors who dragged the sewage stream
That was the Zuck and filtered out the rubble.
(Crater folk lived in a healthy bubble.)
The Crater's intranet accommodated
French and English; bureau bots translated
Content.
      Some who worked above kept phones,
Which died as they descended to their homes.
So Poe stocked stuff that hands could hold;
The silver compact disc, once dross, was gold
Down here. Most Crater folk had been offzuck
Since 2030, when the missile struck.
(The old man certainly gave off that air.)

Between the fourth and fifth, Poe paused, mid-stair-
Well, crossed a gangplank, and arrived beneath
His pod. He climbed a ladder to a wreath-
Emblazoned door, a hatch above his head.
(It was May first. The brittle wreath was dead.)
He didn't like livewood; his old-school door
Was opened by a key. Inside, the floor
He'd climbed up onto was a giant ball's
Interior. It flowed up into walls,
And these kept flowing, curving, and became
The ceiling—all three surfaces the same
And merging smoothly. Poe lived in a sphere,
In short. Above his head, a glass of beer,
Half-finished, faced him like a golden eye
And failed to fall. The beer seemed to defy
Good sense, as did the table it was sitting
On. From where he stood, these things—unwitting
Chandeliers—hung upside down and seemed

To cling to curving ceiling.
                                        Anne had dreamed
Once that the stacks of books and discs that lined
The sphere—the growing piles Poe was blind
To—grew so big they reached towards the centre
Of the sphere, like spokes, and fused. She'd enter
Poe's place and then have to navigate
A globe-shaped wood. Perhaps she'd come to hate
Poe's stuff, she laughed, and this was how her mind
Was telling her. But Poe, who didn't find
It funny, didn't laugh. He hadn't shared
His life in years. Her comment left him scared.

Not that they'd even shared that much, now that
He thought about it. Anne would stay when Cat,
Her daughter, spent the weekend with her dad.
But Anne claimed Poe withdrew. Perhaps he had.
In any case, he found he missed her messes:
Endless unwashed cups; the way Anne's dresses
Wound up draped across his shelves of vinyl;
Her many open books, face down, their spinal
Creases grating on Poe's inner book
Collector; Cat, cross-legged, with the look
A kid gets—open-mouthed—when they're inhaling
Some great tome. Cat loved *The Full-Moon Whaling
Chronicles*, a book about a blue
Whale hunted by a teenage werewolf crew.
Untouched for days, her copy would complain
And cry out with a wolfish howl of pain.

(The author, Mandy Fiction, was a so-called
"Wulf," with fur and fangs. Her fame had snowballed

Since the book's debut. She used to write
For chat salons, her characters a light-
Averse and moody sort: ghosts, vampires,
Werewolves, teenagers—monsters with desires.)

Walking up the wall, Poe crossed the room—
Lights turning on and off and shifting gloom
To other sections of the sphere—and slumped
Down on his couch. He felt a little stumped;
He knew he'd seen the old man's face before.
His head fell back and looked up at his door.
The door, whose hook once held Anne's roiling smart-
Wig, startled—like a wall stripped of its art.

* * *

The next day, flicking lights on, Poe found Cat
Had broken in again. Anne's daughter sat
Upon a crate, against the shelf for "Sci-Fi."
Cat would pick his lock to use his Wi-Fi.

"Hope you didn't scratch the lock this time,"
He said. "Destroying property's a crime."
He took his jacket off.
                              Embroiled in
Her laptop, Cat said, "Hey." The girl was thin,
Her jeans a brand of smartskin: loose right now,
Worn tight at school. Her sweatshirt—*catsmeow*—
Alluded to her ZuckTube zlog. She often
Filmed her day; her mother, forced to soften,
Had allowed the channel in Cat's life.
The need for Wi-Fi was a source of strife,
Though. Cat would surface when she had new work

To upload. Wi-Fi-seekers had to lurk
Outside the Crater; Cat preferred Poe's store.

He counted out the till and walked the floor,
Re-shelving books. He put a track on, "Born
To Be with You," by Dion. Dion's worn
And weary voice kicked in. A minute passed.

Cat looked at Poe. "Who's this?" she said at last.
Without a word, he handed her the case.
She said, "It sounds like he's in outer space
Or something."
                  Graham arrived at nine and stepped
Clean over Cat; they'd all come to accept
Her presence long ago.
                  At ten, she packed
Her stuff to go. She placed a well-thumbed, cracked,
And yellowed paperback in front of Poe.
"So can I borrow this?" A beat-up *Snow
Crash*.
        "Yes," he said. (He knew he'd never see
The book again.) "Bring back the poetry
You've taken, though. You've got a giant stack
At home."
         She zipped her bag and eyed a snack
Bar on the counter.
               Sighing, Poe said, "Take
It."
    "Thanks," she said. And then: "I wanna make
A zlog about the shop."
                 "A zlog?"
                      "We'd do

A tour, I'm thinking. You would take us through.
You'd point out books and records."
                                        Poe looked wary.
"I don't know . . ."
                        "It's like a monastery
In here," Cat said. "People love old shit.
'Poe's keeping all the holy candles lit'
Or something. Plus, you're kind of like a nun."
She put her knapsack on. "We'll make it fun."

* * *

A few days later, running late, Poe found
The old man by the cash. He was astounded.
May, who hated everyone, was *talking*
To the old guy. Laughing. They were mocking
Writers each disliked.
                        "Anne Carson," said
The old man. "*Autobiography of Red*.
She called that book 'a novel in verse.' But it
Was neither!"
                "Well, a piece of fucking shit
Is what it was," May laughed.
                                They talked about
The poetry they worshipped: *This Way Out*
(Starnino), *Groundwork* (Jernigan), *Barista
Bots Translated* (Dunn), *The Scarborough* (Lista),
No End in Strangeness (Taylor), *Paralogues*
(Jones), *A Day's Grace* (Sarah), *Final Zlogs
And Verses* (Arthur).
                        May, amazed, said, "Poe,
This guy's alright."
                        Poe laughed. "It's good to know

You've made a friend at last." He turned to smile
At the old man. "Hi there. Been awhile."

The old man laughed. "I haven't been upslope
This long in years. I'm from the Envelope,
You see."
                    The Envelope—a vast, low cave
Below the fortieth ring—was where the brave
First settlers of the Crater stopped rappelling
And began to set up makeshift dwelling
Spaces. Poe had never been that deep.
The stairwells only went so far, and steep
Walls cut the Envelope off from the Crater
Proper. Several times a year, a freighter
Made the trip down, hovered at the cleft
(A mouth-like rent that ran a mile), left
Supplies, and flew back up. Most scows refused
The fare, and teleporting had diffused
Some bodies through the rock. Not much was known
About the Envelope, which had its own
Strange folk. Some said they worshipped bats and strung
Up interlopers. Others said their young
Were schooled in darkness—in a pitch-black dojo.

The old man said, "I came back for the MOJO."
He held the magazine.
                        Poe nodded, squeezing
Past May, round the counter. "They've been teasing
It for months. It's basically their guide
To great cult artists." Poe unslung his side-
Bag, took up at the cash.
                            The old man placed

The MOJO on the counter's glass and faced
Poe. "I'm just glad to hear Hassid again."
The cover had been changing—Minutemen
One minute and The Vaselines the next,
New artists fading in. The cover text,
However—MOJO's banner—stayed the same.

They chatted for a while. Poe would name
His favourite minor bands and books and movies,
The old man matching him with Flamin' Groovies,
Desperate Characters, and *Two-Lane Blacktop*
(Graham's "amens" a steady aural backdrop).
He said, again, he'd been downslope too long
To count. But once, he'd had a band, whose songs
Were pretty good—before the Crater, years
Ago. It looked as if there might be tears,
But then he smiled. Shook the thought away.
He took his wallet out. "I'd better pay."

Poe rang him through. "The Envelope's so deep.
What brought you up?" He scanned the MOJO. Beep.

The man had come to see a dying friend
And stay a week. But soon he would descend,
Perhaps for good.
                              "I'm just too old to climb,"
He sighed.
                    The door produced its entrance chime—
New customer—so no one noticed when
The MOJO's cover switched to show the men
From Mountain Tea.
                              Poe slid the issue in

A bag. The old man turned to face the bin
Of vinyl, bag in hand.
                              "The holos oughta
Play just fine downslope," said Poe. "I brought a
MOJO home a few months back and found
The music worked. The Zuck links, though, are bound
To die."
                    The old man turned back, grinned, and said,
"It's fine. I've learned to live among the dead."

* * *

Poe sat down on the roof at lunch, his feet
Adangle, thinking he should send a bleat
To Anne. The Crater had evolved an old-
School form of zmail: paper notes were rolled
And sealed with slugs of wise wax, which would read
Your fingerprints. A team of kids would speed
Along the rings and up and down the twisting
Stairwells, knapsacks full of bleats, persisting
Even in the face of snow, which rendered
Rings impassable. A kid surrendered
Bleat to sendee when the wax approved
Their thumb and softened. (Wax remained unmoved
And hard when unknown fingers handled it.)

But what to write? He gazed into the pit
Before him. All around its edge, and looming
Over Poe's shop, condos were assuming
Ever greater views as, floor by floor,
The buildings grew themselves. They seemed to pour
Towards the clouds, each rooftop like a wavy
Hem of liquid inching forward—gravy,

Say, or lava. As their upper edges
Stretched skyward, holes yawned open, lined with ledges:
Windows with a lofty view of Crater.
These new buildings were designed to cater
To a type that yearned to be adjacent
To (but not live *in*) the hole: a nascent
Class of hipster, loathed by Pitizens,
The nickname downslope-dwelling citizens
Preferred. Most Pitizens employed a mix
Of French and English; downslope politics
Demanded both.

     Poe climbed down and went back
To work. He sorted through a looming stack
Of CDs, looked up prices, stickered cases.
Graham went home, then May. Poe put the Faces
On and drafted bleats. He heard a broom
Begin to swish; a maid bot swept the room.

A minor thump: the bot had swung around
And knocked a stack of MOJOs on the ground.
One copy, which had opened up, began
To play a holo of a red-furred man,
Mid-sentence.

    "... Alice X's song, 'Another
Yesterday,' is great, of course. The other
Classic reading of The Mountain, Drew
MacLeod's 'The Dead,' is pretty brilliant, too.
Both songs are just interpretations, though."
The maid bot bent down to retrieve it.

        "No,"
Said Poe. "Just leave it." Poe had not yet browsed
The issue. Plus, like many hearts, Poe's housed

A special place for Mountain Tea. He paused
And watched.
                    The critic, gesturing with paws,
Repeated gossip Poe had heard; like most
Who loved the band, Poe scanned each heated post
That crossed *The Slope*. The *Knot*, which Poe once read
Religiously, was now defunct. It bled
Subscribers when its founder went to prison
And some dude—a Something Donne?—was given
Full control. (Donne's focus—poetry—
Had driven off some fans of Mountain Tea.)
The Slope aside, Poe's current favourite site
Was Cassie Kaye's salon, which placed a light
On Patti Devin's work—beyond the lone
Review for MOJO. Cassie worked alone;
She'd broken with *The Slope* to form a rival
Site, and sparked an overdue revival
In reviewing. Cassie called it *Convent*,
For devoted Pattis.
                    But the content
MOJO's critic shared was old: assorted
Myths about The Mountain's one aborted
Album, fabled iPods full of scraps,
Higashi, monks. The holo went to maps
Of Montréal, 2007—when
James Gordon formed his mythic band—and then
Reverted to the tintype of The Mountain.
He'd seen this pic more times than he could count in
Recent years, but only now—his gaze
On Gordon, to the left, the last few days
Still fresh—did Poe, mouth open, recognize
In Gordon's youthful face the old man's eyes.

11.

From Geoffrey Gibson's *Dreaming Mountain Tea*.
Chapter 3: "A Dream Discography."

The band had broken up in 2012.
They'd voted, three to one, to save and shelve
The master for their debut album, *One*.
But Gordon, odd man out, produced a gun
And tried to make a getaway, the tape
Clutched to his chest, his bandmates' mouths agape.
The bassist wrestled Gordon to the ground
And pinned him. Gordon, crying, said the sound
Was wrong, all wrong. It had to be destroyed.

And maybe it was swallowed by a void
And lost forever in the darkest, bleakest
Timeline. But, in *this* world, Hawks, the weakest
Member of the band, stepped up and stopped
The burning of the tape. The Mountain dropped
All charges; Jim went free.

                              Ten years went by.
Jim sent a note to Hal. "I want to try
To make things right," the postcard, floating in
Hal's eye, had read. "PS. I know I've been

A fool. I promise not to be another
Spector. Please write back. I miss my brother."
Their surnames, Hawks would later tell the press,
Were fakes. The two men shared the last name "Ness."

(Author's Note: Of course, there weren't yet smart-
Eyes in the 2020s. Cut that part?)

The band met up and played the master. Jim
Made peace with what he'd made (though tried to trim
A few imperfect seconds here and there).
A cover was mocked up. A sheet-draped snare—
A ghost. The band gave interviews. They'd gotten
Therapy. They'd made amends. *Forgotten*
Work, their renamed album, finally
Came out—acclaimed—in 2023.

It had the "The Dead" and "Yesterday," plus nine
More cuts. It started with the wobbly whine
Of duelling theremins, as if two flying
Saucers, over rows of corn, were trying
Love songs out. Then Hawks defined a bass line.
Dennis Byrne began to sing of space-time
Woes: how human eyes become eye sockets,
Welling up with rats; how all our rockets
Arc and fall. The track, "A Candle in
The Vacuum," also featured mandolin
By Louis Reid. (He'd taken rock guitar,
On "Yesterday," the second track, as far
As hands on frets could take the form.) The third
Track was "The Dead," the fourth a waltz, "A Word
With God," which blended sitar, horns, and Hawks

On drums. (A hymn to punk song "Chinese Rocks,"
It argued Richard Hell belongs in Heaven.)

The album's next few tracks, from five to seven,
Formed a suite about Van Toorn, the poet
They'd nicked their name from. Those who didn't know it
Would've sworn these string-backed melodies
Were Bach's and not the rock band Mountain Tea's.
The standout, "Lost," was basically a list
Of poets like Van Toorn. A veil of mist,
Suggested by a Moog, grew thicker as
The song wore on. A pair of wheezing jazz
Horns held their notes. And then, as if lopped off,
The clamour stopped. Byrne gave a little cough
And sang the rest alone.
                                         The album's final
Stretch, as fine as sound coaxed into vinyl
Gets, confirmed that Mountain Tea had made
An art-rock monument. As Gordon played
Assorted instruments, from kettledrum
To tuba—and, as Reid began to strum
As though some god had slipped his hands on—Byrne
Reeled off a set of lyrics that would earn
The man a book deal. Gordon sang the last
Song on Side B, "The Living," in a cast
Of mummy plaster, voice a muffled wail.
(The backing rhythm was a loop—a nail
Banged into coffin.) MOJO made it clear:
Forgotten Work was Album of the Year.

Their sophomore effort, *Salvaged from the Silence*,
Was a controversial act of violence

And inspired collage. Throughout the past
Ten years, each member, solo, had amassed
A sheaf of songs: some finished, others but
The slightest shards. Jim took these demos, cut
Them into even smaller bits, then mashed
Them all together. Byrne felt Jim had trashed
Good tracks, but Hawks and Reid stood by the double
Album that resulted. Some saw rubble;
Others heard a work of art—a *Waste
Land*—every sonic scrap and fragment placed
With care. It topped most critics' year-end lists
In 2025.
        Their third disc, *Twists
Of Fate*, was slated to drop soon, but wound
Up taking years. Pursuing some new sound
The band could not explain, with too much cash
And coke, they found they had no shore to crash
Against, no couplet to complete, no box
To work within, no skeleton. Hal Hawks,
Who'd found God, worked on hymns, while Byrne attended
Practice with a fembot, who offended
Like a Yoko Ono. (She'd sit next
To Byrne; the singer wore John Lennon specs.)
Reid made his parts as complex as he could.
Jim forced each session man to wear a hood
And "see" the stave the humid dark revealed.
He wouldn't compromise—and wouldn't yield
To fiscal sense. He purchased Hover Hummers.
Interviewed at least a hundred drummers.
Orchestras were hired to contribute
To a bar or two. Jim would distribute
Homework: albums he expected each

Musician to absorb. He'd try to teach
Them chords no hands could play.
                                        The disc, released
The week the missile landed, was at least
A half an hour too long. The band—outside
The city, touring while two million died—
Were seen as out of touch, their album bloated.
Rolling Stone, which hated Gordon, gloated,
As did other mags whose journalists
Had met with Gordon's censure, spit, and fists.

(Author's Note: By this point, Cloud has spread
Across the globe. Add graf on Cloud? On dead?)

The band regrouped inside a disused truck
Container near the Crater, where they struck
Upon the structure—limits—they'd been lacking.
Recording straight to old-school tape, attacking
Takes, they trusted in simplicity:
Guitars, with Hawks on tom-toms. *Mountain Tea*—
Self-titled, pure, as if they'd reconnected
With some primal self that they'd rejected—
Appeared in 2031, its sleeve
A map of Montréal. Some chose to grieve
By carrying the album underneath
An arm: a badge. Some hung it like a wreath
On pod doors. (Many Crater pioneers
Adored the disc.) The leadoff single, "Tears
Of Rage," by Dylan, was a savvy choice.
The four men sang en masse, one ragged voice,
With Hawks's tom-toms thumping like a heart-
Beat monitor. A distant, scratchy part

By Reid implied a dial being tuned
But catching no clear signal. "Open Wound,"
Another highlight, was a clear allusion
To the Crater. Byrne expressed confusion.
Reid and Gordon played discordant riffs.
The men were sober. Focused. Drug-free. (Spliffs,
Whose smoke once fogged their sessions, weren't allowed
Inside the truck.) The closing track, "The Cloud,"
Was just guitar: a screeching, sprawling squall
That swallowed up the band. It was a wall,
In fact, behind which all four men would duly
Vanish.

      And this time, Mountain Tea would truly
Disappear. They'd made their most direct
Recording; now, they started to deflect
And put on different masks. The band put out
A loud LP attributed to "Lout,"
Their sludge-punk alias. The songs were dirge-
Like, tom-toms drummed with dolls. They would emerge
Again as "Dolphins," playing folk-rock songs
On lutes and banjos. Rumoured gigs drew throngs
Of fans to middles of the bleakest nowhere:
Gutted factories at dawn. Although there
Were no gigs, and most were disappointed,
The songs still offered nourishment. Fans pointed
To Byrne's cryptic lyrics, which some felt
Were dense with clues. Some thought he'd had a pelt
Implanted—went full Post-Man—all because
A song on Lout's LP was called "New Claws."
Some tried to trace the make of rare accordion
That Dolphins used. The must-read fan site *Gordian
Knot* exploded, even as the band

Retreated. Some said Mountain Tea bought land
In Costa Rica. Others guessed that Hawks
Was now a monk, and Reid was tending flocks
Of sheep in Scotland.
                                After '33,
The band became four hermits lost at sea
Inside the minds of fans like Patti Devin.
She wrote a monograph in '37,
The first big work of Mountain criticism,
Doubling as a paean to humanism
For a post-Cloud world of pop and mobs,
Where one man rules the Zuck. "Thus it's the snobs,"
She argued, "who must save us from ourselves.
We need to turn our eyes off, reach for shelves,
And revel in great books and art again.
We need to set our sights on peaks." Amen.

* * *

Chapter 4: "A Dream About the Name."

Let's back up to a time before the fame,
The night the band debated what to call
Itself. Let's be the fly on Gordon's wall . . .

Like all young bands, they bandied names about
All evening. Lou, the lead guitar, liked "Lout,"
A word that clubbed you like a cord of wood.
It's dumb, said Lou, but arty dumb, like blood-
Smeared dolls deployed as drumsticks—Henry Rollins
Does Dada. Jim, on keys, preferred "The Dolphins,"
After the folk-rock ballad by Fred Neil.
Neil's was the sort of myth that would appeal

To men like Jim. His lungs were honeycomb,
His low voice, ladled out. A man must roam
Was Neil's recurring theme. He wrote a few
Great songs, swore off recording, then withdrew
To Xanadu (read: Florida). In exile
For several decades, Neil would not defile
His myth by adding even one more note
Of music to his oeuvre. Like a boat
That's washed its hands of waves but wants to keep
A churning world in view, he chose to sleep
Near water. Sometimes Neil would walk along
The shoreline. Sometimes he would aim a song
At dolphins. Basically, he beached himself,
His rumoured last recordings on a shelf
And out of earshot. But his profile, prow-
Like, always faced the sea.
                    "I think that's how
Great artists—or great bands—should be," said Jim,
As if inside an auditorium
And not his unnamed band's rehearsal space.
"They should be hermits, right? They should efface
Themselves."
                —Excerpted from a manuscript
Found near the author's body, pages clipped
And scattered. Several smarteye tintypes, taken
By the duty guard, suggest a shaken
Snow globe of a space: the author lying
On bare concrete, as a swarm of flying
Coroner bots investigate his cell.
The tintypes, printed, replicate the smell,
And if your eyes pause on a certain detail,
A text box blooms. (The info aids the resale

Of a convict's things.) The ground is deep
With books—*Do Androids Dream of Electric Sheep?*,
The Alteration, *Mountain Tea*—and in
An open *V.*, a bookmark: someone's tintype
Of a green-eyed boy who's waving at
The lens. The duty guard has placed a hat
To blot the author's face. A makeshift cover.
Over this, some armless lenses hover.
Nothing links them; still, they seem to glide
As one: a guardian angel simplified
To wings. A pair of legs (the guard's?) walk through
The scene. The lenses tremble (struggling to
Resist the stirred-up current) but stay near
In hopes that Gibson's eyes will reappear.

12.

Poe's turf-indifferent shoes, a pair of Docs,
Touched down—and barely missed the pointy rocks
That jutted like a growth of dunces' hats.
He let go of the rope and looked up; Cat's
Small body was rappelling down. Her own
Shoes, Converse Basecamps, were as white as bone
And, as they met with rock face, briefly fused
To it. Their treads, chameleons, turned a bruised
And dark-grey colour. As the soles kicked free,
Thin strands of stony rock face stretched like tree
Sap—then snapped back and re-solidified.
(Her passage down had left a wake of dried
And spiny nubs.) She landed next to Poe
And smiled. Thirteen, with a healthy glow
Despite the fact she'd lived her life inside
The Crater. Poe, however, clutched his side
And tried to catch his breath. He hadn't climbed
In years.
        Their shoes and size aside, they rhymed;
She'd pushed for matching ninja jumpers, knit
From nanoweave. "I've got one that'll fit
You," Cat had said that morning. Poe, who'd come
To pick her up, had worn old jeans—a dumb

Pair that would not adjust for temperature
Or weather—and a concert tee. ("The Cure?"
She'd said. "They look like old vampires.") Anne,
Who'd joined Cat at the front door, placed a hand
Upon her daughter's shoulder.

                      "If you *have*
To do this"—she was trying not to laugh—
"You'd better listen. Cat's been climbing since,
Like, three?"

                The girl attempted not to wince.
"Since two," she said, and went to fetch the clothes.

Anne met Poe's eyes, then looked down at her toes.

He leaned against the pod's smooth doorframe. "She'll
Be fine," he said.
               Anne sighed. "I know she will.
It's you who hasn't really climbed in, what,
Ten years?" Her eyes looked at the tee his gut
Had stretched a bit, the face of Robert Smith
A funhouse mirror. "All to chase a myth."

The girl returned, a compact ball of cloth
In one hand. In the other, gloves like sloth
Paws, curving claws extending from each finger.

"That's the jumper?" Poe said.
                    Anne, still linger-
Ing, was laughing, now. Exasperated,
Cat: "It stretches out." She demonstrated.

Poe now watched Anne's daughter yank the rope

Down. Wind it up. They stood on rocky slope
In darkness, dark-blue jumpers giving off
A glow that lit the wall and ground. Poe's cough
Had set the chasm, just below them, hacking.

Mindful of the drop, Cat started tacking
Right, towards a horizontal line
Of distant, glowing light: a slit so fine
And wide it seemed a god had made a rip
Through which a giant envelope might slip.

* * *

Poe had hoped the old man might appear
Again. But weeks had passed. It seemed quite clear
He wasn't coming back. He'd come to see
A dying friend—the guy from Mountain Tea
Had friends!—but said he'd soon descend. Perhaps
For good, he'd added.
                                    Poe examined maps.
To reach the Envelope you had to climb.
He watched a spandexed man on ZuckTube mime
A proper pinch-grip. Cut. The man, still facing
Selfie drone, was on a cliff now, placing
Pitons and, with hammer, demonstrating
How to drive them. "Climbing is creating
Your best self."
                            Poe bleated Anne. "I need
Some help," the bleat said. Poe, prepared to plead,
Was shocked: a short reply by boy came back
An hour later. "Meet at Coffee Hack?
5th Ring?"
                    He looked up from the note and said,

"Reply: Okay!" The boy who'd brought it headed
   Off. You didn't need a note for one-
Word bleats. It cost more, though, to have them run.

Poe found her sipping coffee at a small
Round table, just outside the curving wall
Of liquid glass that held the coffee shop.
Beyond her was a railing. Then, the drop.

He told her everything. To his surprise,
She listened. Mountain Tea. The old man's eyes.
The fact that Gordon—it was him, Poe knew
It—didn't seem to have the faintest clue
His band was famous.
                    "But," said Anne, "he's read
The magazine by now. Perhaps he'll head
Back up?"
            Poe shook his head. "He would've sent
A bleat, I think. To Crater Books. He meant
For that to be his last trip up." He stopped
And looked at Anne. He'd noticed that she'd cropped
Her hair. Was this her moving on? That's when
He tried to say he'd like to try again.

But Anne stepped in and quickly filled the pause:
"My Cat will help. That girl was born with claws."

* * *

The line, as they approached, became a cave:
A long rectangle edged with lights. A grave-
Faced man sat on a stack of shipping pallets.
He wore a cloak and held a pair of mallets.

Sighting them, he stood and struck a gong
To signal: "strangers." It was half the song;
A beat and then a distant gong replied.
He waited 'til the ringing echo died,
And then, still grave-faced, raised a cloak-webbed arm
And waved them in. Around his neck, a charm
Caught light and clarified itself: a bat's
Skull on a chain. Poe nearly jumped, but Cat's
Face leaned in close.

           "Cool necklace, Sir," she said.

"Let's go," Poe hissed. His hand, behind her head,
Steered Cat across the liquid glass that spanned
The cavern's mouth. It trembled like a gland
And sealed behind.

           The ceiling was a strip
Of blue that stood for sky. A tiny chip—
The sky was made of smartpaint—sometimes left
A hole, exposing cave. You'd see a cleft
Cloud, dark and heavy rock behind the gauze.
(The cloud contained a storm of stone.) These flaws
Were minor, though; the strip of sky ran on
And dwindled where the cavern curved. At dawn
And dusk its colour changed, and here and there
It plunged and tapered, forming blue fangs where
It draped stalactite growths. The cavern's walls
Defined a canyon; homes and shopping stalls
Were carved like caves.

           A market filled the first
Third of the Envelope. Small pods, dispersed
Across the next third, sat within a holo
Wood. Beyond: the dojo.

                              "All right, follow
Me," said Cat. She took a step toward
The maze of stalls ahead, a curving sword
Displayed above the first one.
                              "Whoa, whoa, whoa,"
Said Poe. He grabbed her arm and knelt to show
Her what he'd summoned up to stand in for
A stern, authoritative face. "I swore
I'd keep you close. You can't run off, okay?"

Cat frowned. "Your face looks kinda weird that way."

He pressed his hands together, prayer-like. "Cat..."

"Don't worry, Poe." She grinned.
                              The ground was flat
In places, tilting elsewhere. Lights, old Christmas
Bulbs, framed many stalls. One sign said, "Citrus,"
Meaning "Fruit," as "Protein" might mean "Meat"
In upslope gastrostalls. (You had to eat
To stave off scurvy, living this far down.)
The Envelope was like a mid-sized town.
Its stalls were crowded; people—Lopers—wearing
Dark-grey cloaks were milling. Some were staring.

"Let's get going." Poe urged Cat along.

The cave was noisy. They could hear a song,
Some busker's, mingling with the metal clatter
Of the market. To their left, a platter
Of potatoes, floating by, presented;
To its right, a stall that sold fermented

Vegetables, preserves of every kind,
Cured meats, pigs' feet, and pickles. Poe declined
A sample, something on a toothpick, which
An older woman, shrivelled to a witch-
Like narrowness, held out. But Cat took one
And bowed low—just in case that's what was done.

Poe stepped up to a coffee stand's long bar.
He took a stool and eyed a murky jar
Of egg-shaped shadows. Cat flopped next to him
And took her knapsack off. The stall was dim
And lit by several candles, which stirred up
The shadows when the server passed, a cup
Of coffee in each hand. She circled back.

"What can I get you?"

                                      "Coffee," Cat said. "Black."

Poe looked at her, then turned to face the girl
Behind the counter. "Make that two."

                                                              A curl
Of smile crossed the server's face. "Two coming
Up."

              Poe looked around, his fingers drumming
On the counter. Cat took out her Rebel,
Which looked like a phone. A pockmarked pebble,
Resting on its face, demagnetized
And started floating. Cat, who improvised
Her weekly ZuckTube zlog, began to talk
About their morning to the floating, pock-
Marked pebble. In her right hand was the phone
Thing, which she thumbed to move the Rebel's drone

Around. The pebble's golf-ball pocks were tiny
Lens-like apertures. Its fine but spiny
Down was made of microphones too small
To eyeball.
                    Poe had learned that Cat's fourth wall,
Her audience on ZuckTube, had to be
Addressed at times. He didn't mind, though; she
Was helping document important stuff.
For her part, Cat—a kid who had a rough
Idea that locating this old Mountain
Dude would be like stumbling on the fountain
Of youth or yetis—dreamed about the clicks
(Right now, she had 996
Subscribers who'd signed up for *catsmeow*).

"Hey, guys," she said, and scanned her wrist, "it's now
A little after 10 a.m. We've stopped
For coffee." Awkward pauses would be chopped
Out, she'd explained to Poe once. (He'd made mention
Of her lack of script.) It's convention,
Basically, to launch right into talking,
With no sense of where you're going, walking
Down the street or standing at a stand.
A good zlog, Cat stressed, often feels unplanned.

The server set two coffees down. "What brings
You here?" The candles lit two nostril rings.
(The Lopers siphoned power off the Crater;
Candle supplemented generator.)

Slipping off her stool, Cat stepped away
To film. The pebble drone sped up to stay

In front of her. It veered to dodge foot traffic,
Passing through a floating holographic
Sign, which rippled, pond-like.
                              They were on
A quest, said Poe, to find a man who'd gone
To live inside the Envelope a long,
Long time ago. He wrote a famous song,
This man, and wore (and here, Poe swivelled, eyed
The market, gestured with a hand, and sighed)
The same cloak worn by everyone, I guess.
He swivelled back around. A game of chess
Was rising from the counter's smooth livewood,
The pieces steepling upward. (If you stood
Too long beside such wood, it recommended
Fun.) He tugged the white queen, which distended
Like fresh taffy. As he talked, he mashed
It down distractedly.
                              The server splashed
More coffee in his cup and said, "I might
Try Vic. He has his open mic tonight."

"Try Vic," repeated Poe. He turned to make
Sure Cat was not too far, though tried to fake
An interest in some stall.
                              "Your daughter's cute,"
The server said.
                              Poe thought about disputing
"Daughter"—but he let it pass and merely
Said, "Takes after Mom."
                              Cat kept nearly
Crashing into Lopers, pebble staying
Out in front and filming.

                    Poe, still playing
With the chess piece, turned back to the server,
Grimaced, said, "If someone could preserve her
Energy we'd have enough to keep
The Crater lit. This Vic—"
                              "The Bookish Creep,"
She said. "He has a stall down that way." Nodding.
"You hear them in the wood some nights, applauding,
Playing music."
                    Poe just stared.
                                  "The guys
Who sing," she clarified. "It amplifies
Their songs, the way the cavern's shaped down there."

* * *

They found the stall, The Bookish Creep, right where
The market ended. Vic, whose face was chalk-
White, sat behind a rug on which his stock
Of used books rested.
                    "Yeah, we do a thing
At seven. Lopers bring guitars and sing.
We get some poets, too. You're more than welcome."

Vic had Ayn Rand, someone's guide to Belgium,
Naked Lunch, Jack Kerouac—the sort
Of paperbacks designed to briefly court
Young minds; the sort of stuff that stokes and feeds
Rebellious streaks until more grown-up needs
Extinguish them. Cat, thumbing her remote,
Took panning shots, then left the lens afloat
Above a well-thumbed *Catcher in the Rye*,
Whose yellow edges, foxed, had caught her eye.

She snapped a couple tintype stills to add
To Zuckgram; brittle objects brought a sad,
Poetic aura to her feed and got
A lot of likes. A riddle of a thought
In cursive—posted to a wrinkled, tea-
Steeped background—indicated Poetry.

Poe wondered if an older guy named Jim
Attended.
   "Yeah, old Jim, he sings these hymn-
Like things he wrote, like, *years* ago," Vic said,
"While in some upslope band. One's called, 'The Dead'?"

 * * *

They had some time to kill before the open
Mic. Poe didn't want to put his hope in
What Vic said—but very few before
Had come this close. It was the stuff of lore:
To nearly hear the work of Mountain Tea.

"And yet, I think we might've found the key,"
He told Cat's pebble. (She'd insisted Poe
Sit for an interview before the show.)
They sat on stools inside a ramen tent,
Where Poe waxed on, explaining what it meant,
Or would mean, if in fact they got to hear
"The Dead" at last. He sipped a pint of beer;
Cat slurped her noodles. They'd made plans to stay
Out in the holo wood. She'd packed a spray
Tent—basically, a can you shook and sprayed
Across the ground. The foamy mess this made,
A grounded clump of cloud, expanded out

And up, popcorning softly to about
The size of one large igloo.
                            Noodles finished,
They approached the wood. The trees, diminished,
Fit the cave's dimensions: they were tall
As toddlers. Spreading out ahead, the sprawling,
Waist-high wood looked like a patch of ghostly,
Light-blue cabbage. (Here, the cavern mostly
Got its glow from light the trees gave off.
The blue sky also glowed.) Poe paused to cough.
The echo rippled through the cave—and mist
Rose off the trees like rain reversed, consisting
(If you squinted) of a hundred little
Birds. At Cat's approach, the trees would scuttle
Off a bit, the forest parting, breaking,
And resealing. Someone took painstaking
Care to make sure hikers wouldn't stumble
Through the see-through trees, which yielded, humble,
Roots exposed and poised like insect legs.

Soon homes appeared, large pods that looked like eggs
And rose above the trees. Their glowing, rind-
Thick skins, lit by the holos, brought to mind
The eggs that populated caverns in
The 2-D picture franchise *Alien*—
Poe's mind, that is; Cat didn't get the reference.

They found a park, set off a bit in deference
To the pods, and made their camp. Some trees
Were flickering—the fungal bark disease
(Or heart-rot) that afflicts old holos. Kneeling,
Cat sprayed out the tent. This stretch of ceiling

Seemed held up by columns made of flowing,
Holographic water. Each one, glowing,
Pooled to form a placid micro-pond
Whose ripples pulsed like radar. Just beyond
The park, the wood resumed. They'd head towards
A clearing later, following the chords
Of "Long, Long, Long," the Beatles song Vic liked
To play to kick off every open mic.

The foamy tent firmed up, so Poe lay down
Inside to nap while Cat, her face a frown,
Sat on a rock, with laptop, stitching bits
She'd shot. He woke to find her warming grits
She'd bought back at the marketplace. (She'd brought
A camper stove: thin foil with a spot,
An element, that heated up.) They sat
And ate.
          "So *do* you miss Mom much?" asked Cat.
"I mean, since she moved out."
                              Poe looked at her.
Her eyes were on her bowl. The temperature
Had dropped, and so her ninja skin had grown
A peach-like fuzz. He'd never heard this tone
In Cat's voice. Ever.
                    "Course I do," he said.
He felt he ought to hug her; but her head,
Still down, remained engrossed in grits.
                                        "Well, good,"
She said, "Mom might like hearing that." She stood
And looked off in the distance. "Time to go.
It's starting soon." She wouldn't look at Poe.

* * *

They reached a treeless circle edged with stones.
On each stone sat some Lopers. Keg-shaped drones,
With spigots, flew among them, filling up
The cups they held. (Each one had brought a cup
From home.) You peed inside the wood out here,
Which Poe felt strange about. He'd learned to fear
The splash of piss on stony ground, and as
For number twos, he'd yet to bare his ass
To cave air. (Nightly, drones drove through and cleaned
Shit up.)
                   They sat down on a stone. Poe leaned
To try to see if Gordon was among
The hooded, torch-lit faces. Vic had sung
His Beatles ballad, from the circle's centre,
At an organ. Poe watched Lopers enter,
Taking up more stones. No sign of Gordon,
Though. One woman stood and plugged a cord
Into a scuffed guitar. Vic thanked the crowd
For coming out. The woman strummed a loud
And cavern-shaking chord—a blunt transition.

"Now," said Vic, "a brand-new composition.
Please welcome, Abby!"
                              As she stepped
Up to the clearing's centre, having kept
One hand athwart her frets, she started in,
Intoning words like "slit" and "hole."
                                        A thin
Man took a seat across from Poe, his cowl
Up.
        The woman strummed, her face a scowl.

Her hair was short, her pale neck spiky-collared.
Towards the end, she paused a sec, then hollered,
"Matriarchy!"—one fist in the air.
She slashed some chords, her hand a blur, her hair
(Which she had clearly programmed) turning blue
And springing into spikes. When she was through—
Bent double, breathing hard—the crowd erupted.

Vic called up a poet who "disrupted
Consciousness by ditching rules of grammar."
(He would cut up dumbprint mags like *Glamour*
And *The Walrus*, rearranging lines
Of text and, in the process, bourgeois minds.)
Poe looked again; the man who'd entered last
Still wore his cowl.   Half an hour passed.
The sky-blue smartpaint overhead was turning
Orange, which suggested that a burning
Sun was setting. More performers took
The stage. A teen read jottings in a book
(His Moleskine). One sad woman, poised upon
A stool and strumming lightly, sang of dawn
And watching her Inconstant Lover climb
Away, upslope.   And then Vic struck a chime
To signal one last artist. "Thanks for breaking
Bread with us." The cowled man was making
For the organ. "We'll be back next week."

The cowled man, as if to milk mystique,
Sat at the organ and, quite slowly, pulled his dark
Hood down, revealing skin as rough as bark.

It was the old man's face.

                         "Please welcome Jim!"
Said Vic. He clapped his hands. The lights went dim.
The old man's face appeared to float, the fabric
Of his cloak snuffed out.

                     "My favourite maverick
Band, long gone, is Felt," the old man said.
"'All the People I like Are Those That Are Dead'
Was Felt's great song." His face was weathered bone,
But seemed to glow. "I often do my own
Stuff," he continued. "But I'd like to sing
Some Felt." Poe gripped Cat's arm. The pebble thing
Rose up above her head. She thumbed RECORD.

He lifted up a hand. Depressed a chord.
First F, then C, then F. He started playing,
Head down, eyes shut, body slowly swaying.
The swirling organ swelled and filled the cave.
It filled the old man's pauses, wave on wave
Of echo building up, compounding like
A thousand angels crowding round one mic.
His cracked voice echoed through the Envelope.
Poe couldn't move. He felt a small hand grope
For his. Tight grip. He looked at Cat. Her gleaming
Eyes—fixed on the singing old guy, teeming
In the wobbly torchlight—overflowed
And streaked their cheeks with tears: twin lines that glowed
With fire. Overhead, a night sky flickered
Into life. The ceiling's rock self-stickered,
Breaking into stars that signalled evening
In the Envelope.

                   That's when the grieving

Organ's overwhelming wailing stopped.
(It was as if a crying head were lopped
Clean off.) The cave went quiet. Still. A few
Hands started clapping. Loudly. Someone blew
On pincered fingers. Several Lopers rose,
Then several more. They moved in to enclose
The old man. Poe and Cat stood, too, applauding.
The old man shook the hands of Lopers, nodding,
Bowing. That's when his face met Poe's. The face,
James Gordon's, grinned and called across the space:
"My friend! You're here!" He laughed and waved a hand
And said, "Did *you* know people love my band?"

13.

From "Interview with Mountain Tea's Reclusive
Founder: A Special *catsmeow* Exclusive."

We pan across a space, a studio
Apartment, rock for drywall. Jim and Poe
Stand in the very centre.
                      "This is it,"
Says Jim. "My cave. My home."
                              The rock is lit
By glowing statues, standing all around:
A grove. Each one is singing, but is soundless,
Too, poised on a single page ripped from
A magazine. One statue seems to strum
A mute guitar. Another sits and plays
Piano silently.
                 "That's Liam Hayes,"
Says Jim, "the guy behind the rock band Plush."

Poe squats to look. "Great band. They had a lush,
Orchestral sound." Looks up at Jim. "You name
Them in your list of bands that found no fame."

Jim nods. "That's right. I name them in 'The Dead'."

A girl's voice, Cat's, now breaks in overhead.
"It's fitting Gordon loves a band that spent
Years making records no one heard, intent
On being so obscure Plush seemed to be
A dream—like Gordon's own band, Mountain Tea.
Hayes spurned the digital, preferring tape.
Insisting on real strings and horns, he'd scrape
Together what he could and hire session
Men on his own dime. It takes obsession,
Making art, James Gordon likes to say.
Obsession is the artist's only way."

Sharp cut to medium shot: the two men sitting
On a threadbare sofa. Bats are flitting
Overhead, the ceiling studded with
Stalactites.
       "What I loved," says Jim, "was myth.
I thought it should be hard to hear a band.
It ought to take some work. So I'd demand
Our stuff—*The Dead*, say—only be on vinyl."
Mock-stern: "'Has to be my way! That's final!'"
Cut to the holo statues. "That's what I
Admired"—the shot now zooms in on the eye
Of Hayes—"Artistic limits. Stricture. Vision."
Up close, the eye is snowy television,
The holo's resolution breaking down.

Cut back to Poe on sofa, with a frown.
"You tore the pages out..."

Jim laughs. "Of course!
I muted them. They make a lovely source
Of light when one lives in a cave."

Poe smiles,
Presses on. "Some place you next to Miles,
Dylan, Spector. What's it like to find
Out people love The Mountain?"

"I don't mind,
I guess." Jim pauses. "But I wish they'd heard
The songs." He looks at Poe. "It seems absurd,
You know?"

Poe spreads the page about The Mountain
On the ground. It froths and plumes a fountain
Made of light; the man-sized, red-furred talking
Head resolves and launches in. Jim, balking
At the holo, waves a hand: oh please.
The critic, though, keeps going: ". . . Mountain Tea's
Cult following continues to explode."
A map of Earth fades in, a pulsing node
On every continent. "Its reach extends
Across the world." An arrow lengthens, bends,
And joins the nodes. The map begins to curl
And form a globe—which shrinks down to a pearl
And dots the single "i" in "Mountain Tea."

Jim snorts. "What bullshit hagiography."
He looks straight at the lens. "I hope that's not
What *this* is."

Poe says no. "But look, the *Knot,*
The Slope—their sheer existence doesn't *move*
You?"

    "Well," says Jim, "I think these fan sites prove
The Zuck's a waste of time."

                                Poe takes a sheaf
Of paper out. "I want to read you"—leafing
Through—"a part from *Dreaming Mountain Tea*.
The 'he' is you. '[H]e spurns reality,
Composes parts for banjo. Singing dog.
(Dreaming's better; making art's a slog.)'"
Poe pauses.

                    Jim just shakes his head. "I mean,
It's silly, this fan fiction stuff. I've seen
The Zuck encourage worse, though. Patti Devin
Was driven off way back in '37,
Right? My friend, who wrote the piece that made
Me famous? Lovely girl. Those fuckers flayed
Her. Chased her down here. Good for us, I guess."

Poe looks confused. "You knew her? Patti?"

                                                    "Yes,
Of course," says Jim. "She lives above, inside
The Crater. Lived, I mean. Last month, she died."

* * *

The film goes black. A couple tintype stills
Of Patti pass across the screen. Cat fills
In gaps, explaining that the critic fled
The Zuck (some mob was gunning for her head)
And got as off-grid as a girl can get:
Got downslope. "Patti wanted to forget
And be forgotten. Little did she know
She'd meet James Gordon." Cut to shots of snow

Inside the Crater, layering the rings
Like icing. Patti with a shovel. Strings—
Stock music—swell behind a vibraphone.
More shots, from overhead, suggest a drone.
We get a glimpse of Patti standing with
James Gordon. Neither knows they're part of myth;
They're making faces—scuppering their pose.

A book fades slowly in: *Collected Prose*
Of Patti Devin, edited by Cassie
Kaye, with art by Seth: a pretty classy
Object. Cat: "But Patti never knew
That Authors for a Safer World was through
By 2039. She never thought
That honest criticism, which she fought
For, would return—and never thought her biting
Prose would find some readers, that her writing
Would survive. She took a teaching job
Inside the Crater, where the onzuck mob
Offended by her pieces had no reach.
She knew her craft, and found she loved to teach
A writing class to children."
                                            Sitting on
A stone, Jim watches as a holo swan
Glides clean through cavern floor. He starts to talk.
"I taught a music class—Forgotten Rock—
From time to time inside the Envelope.
Patti and her colleagues came by rope
Once—basically a kind of missionary
Thing. Us Lopers can be somewhat wary.

"But I liked her. Patti couldn't shake

The feeling that she knew me. Didn't take
Her long to figure out just who I was."

Low cello. Cat takes over. "But because
They both lived downslope, neither knew her piece
Had sparked a cult. She'd later pass, quite peace-
Fully, age sixty, in her home, eighth ring.
For years, she'd been about the only thing
That drew the great auteur out from his cave."

* * *

Dissolve to Jim, framed in his door. "My grave,"
He says, and sighs, and beckons-in the camera.
"Needs a dusting." Cut to panorama
View of cave. Beyond the MOJO holos,
There isn't much.

        Cat's floating pebble follows
Jim, who goes about his standard day.
He looks upon his shelves and seems to weigh
Which record he should play. He straightens up
The blanket on his mattress. Cleans the cup
(He owns but one) he drinks his coffee from.
Wears earphones, eyes closed, and begins to hum.
He steps outside the cave to find a child
With a bag of food, her hair a wild
Thatch. "Merci," he says.

        Cat's voice resumes
As Jim scoops beans out of a can. She zooms
In on the artist eating. "Gordon lives
A simple, stripped-down life. He mostly gives
His time to teaching music at the dojo,
Reading" (shot of Gordon browsing MOJO),

"And mingling with the people he now calls
His family" (shot of Gordon browsing stalls
Inside the market, nodding to his fellow
Lopers). "No longer full of rage, he's mellow
Now."
            Dissolve to Jim, who's standing in
The holo wood. A sawing violin
Suggests reflection. "At the time, I hated
Critics. No one got what I'd created.
'He's a warden,' someone wrote. It rhymed
With 'Gordon.' Clever motherfuckers slimed
My name—" He stops. "But maybe they were right."
He tries to touch a treetop, leafed with light;
It scuttles off. "The Mountain *was* confined.
But what a noise it made inside my mind."

* * *

"But what exactly did James Gordon do
For all those years before the Crater drew
Him in?" To answer that, Cat starts to list
Off jobs he's had: grad student, anarchist,
Unloader of assorted hover trucks,
And drifter—jobs to suit a life in flux.

Then Gordon, like Fred Neil, the folkie, found
His way to southern Florida. He wound
Up washing dishes in a seaside dive
That specialized in mussels, fights, and "live"
Performances—Cat's stress on "live," an eyebrow
Raised ironically, a slightly highbrow
Tone now creeping in.
                        "They'd set up near

The back," says Gordon, "but they'd disappear,
At last call." They were juke bots, four projections
That could play most hits or take directions
From the crowd. Their bodies, see-through, glowed—
But fluttered when their bulbs were old, and snowed
Like detuned televisions when they dropped
The Wi-Fi.
             One night, closing, Gordon mopped
His wary way towards an old, unplayed
Piano at the back. The thing was made
Of wood, not light, and fingers hadn't pressed
Its keys in years. He took a seat—to test
How it might feel to play a melody.
The owner, at the till, looked up to see
Her recent hire hunched and conjuring
A mournful ballad. Gordon started singing.

When he paused, she clapped. You oughta play
More often.
           Gordon laughed her off. You say
That now . . .
             A couple weeks went by. One night,
He found himself chitchatting with the light
Bulbs—what professional musicians call
Such toys, notes Cat. The light bulbs were in thrall.
A couple held guitars. One manned a kit.
Their gear was made of light; the sweat and spit
The juke bots shed when they performed were weightless
Sparks. Two speakers (mounted on a plate
Screwed to the wall) produced the actual sound
The juke bots seemed to make, while on the ground,
A bulb-embedded ball produced the bots

And filled their holographic heads with thoughts.
The ball's AI provided all the brains,
But Gordon faced the juke bots, taking pains
To speak to each, as if the holos had
Distinctive, bounded minds. And they were glad—
Or rather *it* was glad, the AI in
The ball—to listen to this aging, thin,
And flesh-based man, who quoted poetry
And once led something he called "Mountain Tea."
Throughout this sequence, Cat's been leaning on
Stock tintypes: bars, pianos, skies at dawn.

"The owner, sitting on her barstool, kept
An eye on me," he says. "We hadn't slept
Together yet."
                    He walked the bulbs through songs.
His voice would rise, as if addressing throngs.
Let's try a take, he'd say. The holo band
Would start to play. He'd quickly raise a hand.
Too slow, he'd say, or it should sound like loons
In anguish. He was teaching them his tunes.

They're beautiful, your songs, the owner said
A little later. She had heard "The Dead"—
Though didn't know it—plus some tracks intended
For The Mountain's album, tracks that wended
In directions and through chords no ear
Had heard in years. Her eye disclosed a tear,
In Gordon's telling. What you've made is art,
She said.
                "I said she had a lovely heart
And walked towards her." As he crushed her lips

To his, the juke bots played a song called "Ships
In Bottles," which, Cat mentions, would've closed
The unmixed album. Gordon had composed
It for a dozen strings; they multiplied,
The bots, to twelve. Their empty claws implied
The necks of ghostly violins. The AI
Tried to make the sound that strings make.

                                   May I
Have this dance? he asked her when she broke
Off from the kiss. The strings grew more baroque.
The couple waltzed around the empty dive.

Weeks passed. He found he liked to teach. The hive
Mind that the juke bots shared had learned his set
List. They had grown into a crack octet:
The auteur manned the old piano, while
His juke-bot band—instructed not to smile—
Played vibes, guitars, a drum kit, strings, and double
Bass. The owner liked to call him "Trouble."
She'd started sleeping in his rented room.
She was the sort of moth that's drawn to gloom;
His window looked upon an empty pool.

But after shift one night, perched on her stool,
She said, why don't you play a show? You guys
Can do it here.

                   He didn't meet her eyes.
He sat before the keys, head down.

                               "'Yeah, maybe'—
What I told her. Then my bulbs did 'Baby
Blue'—the Beach Boys song. Our last. I went
Home by myself that night. Said I was spent

Or something. She was cheerful. 'Maybe next
Time'."
          In his rented room, he scrawled some text
Across his only copy of *The Dead*:
Two words, "I'm sorry," on the sleeve, in red
And ragged marker. Early in the morning,
Gordon left the single, as if mourning
Something with a wreath, against the front
Door of the dive—he figured it was blunt
Enough—and stepped into a Zuber not
Long after. He had read that those who sought
Adventure were exploring Montréal's
New Crater. Shots of caverns, waterfalls,
And B-roll of a Loper in a hood.
Dissolve to Gordon in the holo wood.

* * *

Poe's voice, off-screen, ahems. "What happened to
The restaurant owner and the juke bots who
Had learned to play your songs?"
                              James Gordon shrugs.
"She likely would've wiped the bots." Small bugs—
The mist of micro-birds above the waist-
High treetops—swirl about. "Why would she waste
The memory?"
              Poe asks, "So what about
The single?" (Cat breaks in, to gloss the drought
Of Mountain content, splicing in some shots
Of deserts, sun-cracked plains, and Edmund's bot's
Destruction of the only extant copies.)

Jim laughs. "I guess you're hoping I have floppies?"

(Cat breaks in to give an overview
Of floppy disks; she'll pause the interview
A few more times, to help the audience
Along.) "I haven't seen a copy since—
Well, Florida. The label didn't press
That many."

                Off-screen, Poe says something.

                                    "Yes,"
Says Jim, "we cut an album, but again…"
The trees part as he walks.

                     "The other men
In Mountain Tea are gone now," Poe says sadly.
Here, Cat holds the take.

                    "I loved them madly,"
Jim says at last. "I miss them every day.
We weren't together long, but when we'd play
A song, we'd mesh our minds. The magazine's"—
He stops; a stock track, oboe, intervenes—
"The magazine's the first I'd heard. It's hard
To"—something in his throat—"it's like a shard
Shoved in your heart, to read about your friends"—
The trees close up behind—"who met their ends
So long ago. I didn't have the slightest
Clue."

* * *

      The screen fills up with green, the brightest
It has been. Cat says, "A stretch of sky
Is out"—we're in night vision, which is why
The green—"but Mountain Tea's ex-leader leads
Us deeper into darkness, to the seeds
Of Montréal's bright future."

                    Jim and Poe
Are walking through the cave. Their bodies glow
A radiated green. Cat's voice sounds British,
Accent creeping in. Perhaps the finish
Of the documentary needs a certain
Air?
             They reach a giant wall of curtain,
Rippling fabric flowing up to form
A dome. The curtain seems suffused with warm
Light from within. It's like a massive bird-
Cage, draped in cloth, the shapes inside it blurred
And moving. Once they reach the curtain, though,
It's clear the flowing cloth's freestanding; no
Cage undergirds the structure. Cat turns off
Night vision. Jim walks up, pretends to doff
A hat. A corner of the curtain peels
Toward them. Once they're in, the tent reseals.

Interior shot. The two men stand inside
The dome. The cloth, a strain of living hide,
Resembles circus tent. Kids run around,
At play. A few are lying on the ground
And reading. Grown-up Lopers circulate.
A couple kids mount milk crates to debate
Each other; other kids, cross-legged, sit
And watch and holler things. The space is lit
By lanterns overhead, which look like beach
Balls, floating.
                    British voice resumes: "They teach
The children of the Envelope in here."
Two kids swarm Jim, their skin so pale it's clear,
Their veins a roadmap. "After years of aimless

Wandering, James Gordon made a name
Below the vanished land he'd once lived on.
At loose ends and approaching fifty, drawn
To life inside the Envelope, he found
The perfect crypt to keep a cult band's sound:
A place that's off the grid of someplace that's
Already off the grid, the wings of bats
Providing the applause. And yet, despite
His moodiness, he learned to be a light
For others."

         Cut to Jim, who slowly walks
Amid a group of children stacking blocks.
He points at one lone girl, who seems to stare
Straight through him as she draws upon the air.
But no one else can see the lines her pen
Appears to scrawl. Cat breaks back in again.

"This trend is common: Loper kids with smart-
Eyes, coping with the sunless sky through art.
They sketch a circle in the upper-right-
Hand corner of their gaze. It gives no light
But stands in for the sun and stays in view
No matter where they move their eyes. In lieu
Of darkness, they have found a canvas."

* * *

Cut back to Jim and Poe, who stroll the campus
Just outside the dojo. On the crack-
Lined plain of rock, against the curtain's back-
Drop, stands a keyboard. Jim, without a word,
Sits down, as Poe steps out of frame.

         "The nerd

Inside my heart," says Jim, "is still alive.
He plays piano every day. They drive
The children from the tent and sit them down."
He smiles to himself. "Of course, I clown
Around a bit. 'Down by the Bay'—that kind
Of thing." The smile fading. "But I find
I like to play forgotten work by bands
Like Shack or Rocket from the Tombs"—his hands
Begin to form stray chords—"or Johnny Thunders.
Lawrence. Flipper. Dexys Midnight Runners.
Kevin Shields. James Booker. Chris Bell. Plush.
The House of Love. Graham Coxon. Deaf School. Lush.
Pere Ubu. Slint. The Slits. Jean-Claude Vannier.
Pete Ham. The Sonics. Andrew W.K.
The Adverts. Godz. The La's. The Seeds. Scott Walker.
Mary Margaret O'Hara. Jarvis Cocker.
Thelma Houston. Gordon Anderson.
The Pastels. Cotton Mather. Robert Quine.
Judy Henske. Love. The Blue Ox Babes.
Karen Dalton. Raspberries. Nick McCabe.
Nick Drake. The Chocolate Watchband. Dennis Wilson.
Paul Westerberg. The Placemats. Alex Chilton.
Peter Laughner. Can. The Vaselines.
The dB's. Talk Talk. Ocean Colour Scene.
Arthur Lee. Fred Neil. The Seeds. Big Star.
The Aliens. The Beta Band. James Carr.
Lost Americas. The Raincoats. PiL.
The kids love Denim."

        Poe, off-screen, says, "Will
You play 'The Dead' for us? I'm told you play
It sometimes."

        "Well, I do, but not the way

We used to play it." Jim looks at the keys.
"I don't remember all the words. Brain freeze,
Or maybe just old age. It's been so long.
I've got the chords still. But I do the song
With Patti's words now."

There's a pause, then Poe
Says, "Patti's words?" Behind, the dojo's glow,
A warm white light, now toggles to the red
Of Broadway curtains.

"Yes, I play 'The Dead',"
Says Jim, "but use the words from her review."
He laughs. "At this point, well, it's her song, too."
An unseen drone, above, turns on its spot-
Light.

"It's a bat," says Cat, "half-bat, half-bot,
To be precise." She offers up some stats
About the mating habits of the bats
And just how many populate the blue-
Skinned rock above. She tilts her camera's view
To show a twitchy, living pelt that seems
To cling to clear-blue sky. "They fire beams
Out of their eyes," says Cat. Her camera follows
Lines of light, connecting bats to holos.
The bats, it seems, project the vegetation.
"They grow the trees and recharge at a station.
The ones out here, the dojo's specimens,
Have learned to treat its tiny denizens,
The children, as their charges, putting light,
Like this, on those who've wandered into night."

James Gordon, sitting in his spotlight, sighs.
His fingers find some chords. He shuts his eyes

And starts in: "Over reverbed brass and strummed
Guitar, as choral cowboy voices hummed
Spaghetti-Western-style, the singer read
A list of lost, neglected bands in dead-
Pan: 'Felt' (pause), 'Plush' (pause)—each pause punctuated
By piano chord. The choir abated,
Giving way to H.U. Hawks's bass,
A pulse that emphasized the empty space
It echoed in. Two vintage theremins
Began to moan. A ghost—George Harrison's?—
Possessed guitarist Louis Reid and made
Him play a riff a Beatle might've played,
A spectral solo that was mesmerizing,
Masterful, low strings now slowly rising,
Singer Dennis Byrne imploring—crying—
'Raise the dead'!"

                              Poe, head down, is trying
Not to cry. (Cat's swung the lens around.)
He waves her off, but now it seems she's found
A better shot: beside Jim's feet, a shoot
Has bloomed. A holo tree has taken root.

She wonders if it's too contrived a symbol.
Poe would balk when drummers tapped their cymbals
Too emphatically, when writers under-
Scored their points. He'd rail against such blunders,
Back inside his store: the weighted wink,
The malleted motif. He didn't think
His staff paid much attention. Cat did, though.
She loved his rants. "You've got to earn your snow
On headstones," Poe would say of Joyce's story

"The Dead." Although the snow risked being hoary,
Joyce had earned the image by the end.

The holo shoot she's filming starts to bend
A bit, as if a sapling made of light
Could bow to gravity. Perhaps it's trite,
The sapling, but she can't resist such signs
Of life. The sapling starts to sprout two lines—
A pair of holo branches, drawn by beams,
Unfurling fast like time-lapse limbs in dreams.

As Jim plays on, the hidden bat above
Imagines leaves and places them with love.

Epilogue.

The Shiba Inu walked itself each night.
The neighbourhood was dark, a single light
Above each door. Each house was set an arm's
Length from the next; a mix of bungalows, barns,
And townhomes pressed to form a checkerboard
(The claustrophobic grid, some giant's hoard).
There were no roads; the arm's-length space between
The homes suggested paths, and these were green,
Long strips of pixieturf. From overhead,
They made a latticework of lanes that spread
Toward four distant walls. (The Shiba's bark
Was coughed back by these walls.) The sky was dark
And low and stripped of stars. The bunched-up homes
Looked like the maverick work of tricksters: gnomes
Who'd plotted out a town too dense to walk.
Adults would need to sidle, but could knock
On two front doors at once, or, if they spun,
Touch four homes where two laneways met as one.

But humans never walked among the houses—
Just the Shiba. It could hear a mouse's

Heartbeat several blocks away, a squeaking
Like a chew toy's. Seconds later, streaking
By, the Shiba was a blur, and where
The mouse had been, a mist of blood and hair.
This almost never happened, though; most mice
Steered clear.
                    The Shiba walked the laneways twice
A night and counted up the homes and checked
Its count against the system's. White but flecked
With grainy dots, the Shiba was a plastic
Model that could stretch and turn elastic,
Or press through a fence, its body bulging
Forth as Play-Doh worms, the fence divulging
Dog. Its black-tipped nose produced a kind
Of sonar ping, which filled its doggy mind
With all the shapes and structures it would have
To navigate. It sometimes split in half
Where laneways intersected, sending two
Dogs, smaller ones, down separate lanes to do
Two tasks.
                    From time to time, old homes would trade
Their spots with newer ones. They'd start to fade
And leave a gaping hole within the grid;
This meant a realtor bot had placed a bid
And bought a property. (The homes were mostly
Empty: vintage pieces.) Soon, the ghostly
Outline of a new home needing storage
Would define itself, and milky porridge—
Molecules amassing—would fill in
The fizzing, house-shaped frame. A thunderous din

Announced the change, the atmosphere adjusting
As new matter muscled in, a gusting
Sleet that turned to sludge and then to brick.

One day, the dog, out running, sensed a flicker
Of the faintest life inside a brand-
New guest: an old Victorian, unmanned,
According to the manifest. It hunched
Before the door and mashed its face, which bunched
Like clay, against the keyhole. On the other
Side, inside the darkened house, another
Dog assembled, slowly, from the paste
The hole expressed. The dog, now solid, raced
Around the house. Its brain was set to ROAM,
Its eyes were bulbs, its tail a metronome.

And in an empty fireplace, the Shiba
Found the lifeforms it had sensed: amoebae,
Which had grown inside the carcasses
Of what the Shiba's crack analysis
Determined to have been some bonsai goats.
The Shiba sniffed around, two beams of motes
Projecting from its eyes, recording all
The corpses.
                    On the ground, against one wall,
A painting stood—one of a few things still
Within. The Shiba's mind began to fill
With thoughts; it merely had to be inside
A house and, click, the owner's name would slide
Right into place. This home had once belonged
To E. Higashi, businessman, who longed
To be a mountaineer and worshipped tea.

A record player on a killing spree
Had killed Higashi with a pen. ("The Pen
Proves Mightier Than the Sword," from *Mountain Men*,
A site that seemed to be for other fans
Of tea, described the killing.) Several scans
Of Zuck—the dog maintained a link—enabled
It to snag more facts. He'd sought a fabled
Teabag: Dead Tea. Plus, the painting clearly
Was Higashi: someone trying dearly
To look poised. Composed. The Shiba matched
It to a tintype from his funeral, snatched
By something called *The Slope.*
                                        The Shiba cocked
Its head, its tail a blur; its nose had blocked
New shapes behind the canvas: one appeared
To be a square, a sleeve of dumbboard sheared
From tree flesh, and, inside, a disc of what
Would seem to be black vinyl, with a rut—
A single groove, quite fine—that ran around
The disc in gyres and contained pure sound,
Or anyway that's what the Shiba, rooting
Through the Zuck, had learned. It made a hooting
Noise, the vinyl circle, when you faced
A record player bot and, stretching, placed
The thing, a halo, on its open head.

The Shiba's X-ray picked out words in red
("I'm sorry," scrawled in cursive on the dumb-
Board sleeve) and smaller printing ("Guess I'm Dumb,"
"Bangkok") on images of other sleeves
Inside a scow port.
                                Sometimes, non-dog thieves

Would scour homes like this to find lost stuff.
The Shiba made a metal sound—"Ruff ruff!"—
And summoned up a manifest: the whole
Supply of homes, recorded on a scroll,
Which only its eyes saw; a doc that floated
In midair. The dog barked twice. This noted
Two additions: one, the painting, two,
The disc behind the canvas, out of view.
It was, the Shiba barked, a work of art
Within a work of art. Please send a cart
And order an appraisal.
                                    Once outside,
The dog resumed its standard sprint. Its hide
Displayed a diamond-shape: the logo for
The Zuber service Kite. On every floor
Inside the Kite HQ, a neighbourhood—
A grid of mashed-together houses—stood,
The sky above a ceiling. Dogs patrolled
These neighbourhoods, did counts of homes, unrolled
Their manifests, and had no clue that they
Were in an eighty-storey cube of grey
Concrete. The cube's immense unfriendliness
Was sharpened by the lovely emptiness
Of rural Edmonton, whose fields were pretty:
Green and vast. The cube looked like a city
Of the future, as depicted in
A concept sketch.
                                    A rocket with a fin
That said "DTJR" would soon erase
It, though. The cube would reappear in space,
Along with much of greater Edmonton's
Terrain and bedrock: many megatons

Of earth, scooped from the ground. The earth would keep
Its bowl shape for a beat, then drift and seep
Into the larger Cloud, like silt suspended
In a base, unfurling 'til it blended
In. The cube, afloat within the storm
Of exostuff, would hold its basic form
A little while yet. Incoming matter—
Marbles, bikes, old sinks—would start to batter
It.
    The acting president—still "acting"
After many years and now reacting
To a lack of jobs—had launched a second
Terra-missile. (He had failed to reckon
With the failures of the first.) The missile,
On its way, produced a high-pitched whistle,
Which the Shiba things and mice could hear,
Their ears alert.
               They'd all soon disappear.
The whining missile, meant for someplace far
Away, was falling like a flaccid star
Toward the cube, which held the house, which held
The painting and its secret. All would meld
Inside the Cloud, in which the random, jumbled
Cast-offs of the planet slowly tumbled
Like the contents of a diorama
Dumped in space. A poster of Obama.
A sideboard, open like a bomb bay, doors
Disgorging china, silverware. Three drawers,
Ejected from their dresser, drifting by
As life rafts do. A bot-barista's eye,
Gouged from its head and trailing filaments:
A jellyfish. Old pixiepaper prints

Of Munch and Miró. Armless lenses—wings
Of glass—in aimless flight. Two napkin rings,
Too small to ever hula hoop a Saturn.
MOJOs. Scows. A blinking, dying lantern.
Writing desks. Their quills. Rejected thoughts.
A flyer for a reading. Trussed-up bots.
A pane of liquid glass, pocked with debris.
Remaindered books. Self-published poetry.
Assorted frozen bodies with their souls
Sealed in. Assorted critics, fanboys, trolls,
Musicians, writers, and historians.
The walls that once composed Victorians,
Adrift like disassembled gingerbread.
And one last spinning copy of *The Dead*.

Acknowledgments.

Thanks to Daniel Brown, Brooke Clark, Evan Jones, Michael Lista, Rick Ramdeen, and Carmine Starnino.

Thanks also to the brilliant poet Amanda Jernigan, who said I needed a mechanic, and duly tightened all the bolts. She deserves her own cult following.

My wife, Christie, provided love, patience, and encouragement; *Forgotten Work* wouldn't have been possible without her. My son, Henry, furnished the necessary naps—several years' worth—in which the book was written.

The birth of my daughter, Annie, gave me a deadline.

Jason Guriel is the author of several
collections of poems and
a book of essays. He lives in Toronto.